HEIRESS'S
PREGNANCY
SCANDAL

HEIRESS'S PREGNANCY SCANDAL

JULIA JAMES

MILLS & BOON

First published in Great Britain 2019
by Mills & Boon, an imprint of HarperCollins*Publishers*
1 London Bridge Street, London, SE1 9GF

Large Print edition 2019

© 2019 Julia James

ISBN: 978-0-263-08249-4

MIX
Paper from
responsible sources
FSC
www.fsc.org   FSC® C007454

This book is produced from independently certified
FSC™ paper to ensure responsible forest management. For
more information visit www.harpercollins.co.uk/green.

Printed and bound in Great Britain
by CPI Group (UK) Ltd, Croydon, CR0 4YY

For WSW—my cosmology advisor!

CHAPTER ONE

NIC FALCONE STEPPED through the service door into the casino, glancing around with a deeply satisfied sweep. Yes, this had been a good idea, acquiring and restoring this fading *hacienda*-style hotel deep in the western desert, yet still within reach of both Las Vegas and the West Coast. Another prestigious money-spinner for the global Falcone chain of luxury hotels. More glittering proof of just how far he'd come in his thirty-odd years—from the backstreets of Rome to being one of the richest men in Italy.

The fatherless slum kid who'd started his first job at barely sixteen in the basement—literally—of the fabled Viscari Roma hotel had, by his own gruelling efforts, climbed as high as that dilettante playboy Vito Viscari, who'd had a legendary hotel chain handed to him on a plate by his family.

Nic's expression shadowed as he remembered. Through dogged hard work he'd worked his way up through the ranks at the Viscari Roma, every promotion striven for, until he had finally been in line for the big move into management that he had *known* he was totally qualified for.

But Vito's uncle, the chairman of the company, had instead preferred that his inexperienced nephew—fresh out of university, with none of the hard-earned, hands-on track record that Nic had under his belt—should get a taste of his future inheritance.

Nic had been passed over—and from that moment he'd known that from now on he would work only for himself. The seeds of the Falcone hotel chain had been sown. Falcone would be the rival that would outsoar Viscari once and for all.

And through a level of hard work that had absorbed his whole life Nic had succeeded— fantastically. So much so that last year he had been able to swoop, like his namesake the predatory falcon, to take ruthless advantage of an internal power struggle within the divided Viscari family and snap up an entire half of the Viscari portfolio of hotels in a blatantly hostile acquisition.

It had proved, though, to be a triumph that had turned to ashes. Yet again Nic had felt the pampering hand of nepotism thwarting him. This time it had been, of all things, Vito's mother-in-law, persuading Nic's own investors, who'd funded his acquisition, to sell the hotels back to her so she could hand them over to her son-in-law, Vito.

Yet again Vito had prospered without lifting a finger for himself—thanks to help from his family.

But the determination that had lifted Nic from the backstreets had kicked in again, and in the months since losing his grip on the Viscari portfolio he had reacted by lining up a string of potential new Falcone properties, including this, the newly opened Falcone Nevada, with its oh-so-lucrative on-site casino.

His keen eyes swept the crowded gaming floor as he strolled forward, noting that a good few of the gamblers had likely come over from the conference wing of the hotel, where a gathering of astrophysics academics were holding their annual shindig. Including the cluster of young hopefuls now quitting the bar area to head to the gaming floor. Leaving behind a woman who was now raising a hand to them in a casual goodnight.

A woman who halted him in his tracks. Tall, graceful and dazzlingly blonde.

Every sense went on high alert. In his time he'd seen—and sampled—many, many beautiful women. But none like this. He felt his stomach muscles clench, held his breath. His eyes fastened on her. And desire—hot, intense and instant—quickened...

Fran watched the post-grad students go off to buy their chips and hoped they wouldn't lose their shirts at the tables. They were clearly in demob happy mood and making the most of this, the final night of the conference. As for herself, she should head off, for she still had a poster session to give the following morning, before the plenary session, and it wouldn't hurt to run through her presentation again.

But as she turned back towards the barman to call for her bill a voice behind her spoke.

'No temptation to try your luck at the tables?'

It was a deep voice, with an American accent that did not sound western, and it held a gravelled timbre that made her turn.

And as she did so her eyes widened.

Oh, wow...

The silent exclamation, as instinctive as it was unstoppable, resonated in her consciousness.

The man who stood there, his pose deceptively relaxed, was tall—easily topping her own willowy figure—with broad shoulders, lean hips and a muscled chest that looked as if it could take a punch without even noticing.

In fact, she registered, in her subliminal sweep of his features, it looked as if his nose, set in a face that was hard-planed and strong-jawed, had been on the receiving end of a slug at some stage.

The slight bump was a flaw that only added to his powerful appeal. The man might be in a tux, but everything about him said *tough*.

Part of the security team here? she wondered, a mind still reeling from the visceral impact he'd made on her. It had been like walking into a wall—a wall she'd never seen coming.

For a second—a sub-second—she was frozen, taking him in, reacting to him on a level at which she never, just *never*, reacted to men. Not even the formidably good-looking Cesare, the man she had so nearly married, had had the overpowering instantaneous impact the man standing here now was having on her.

He's nothing like the men I usually find attractive!

With the exception of Cesare, with his hawkish, aristocratic demeanour, she'd always only gone for men with studious looks—not the muscled type that she'd always regarded as... well, *brutish*.

But there was nothing brutish about this man. Not with eyes like that. Glinting with sharp intelligence.

And blue—piercing blue—which is really weird, because the tan of his skin tone and the sable of his hair indicates Hispanic, probably...

Yet even as she made that reasonable assumption she realised she needed to do something other than just gaze dumbstruck at him. Should she acknowledge his remark? Without vanity, she knew from experience that her blonde looks drew male eyes—and more—and if she was chatted up she normally kept her reaction vague to the point of evasive until she could get away or the man gave up. If absolutely necessary she froze them out.

For the moment, though, she went for option one, and gave a brief, impersonal flicker of a smile and a demurring shake of her head.

'Not my thing…gambling,' she replied, glad to accept the leather-bound drinks bill, and jot her room number on it.

'You're part of the conference?'

Again, the deep, slightly gravelled voice made her glance up as she pushed the folder back to the barman.

'Yes,' she acknowledged.

She moved to slip off the high stool, and immediately the man's hand was there, guiding her. She glanced at him, murmuring her thanks, but wished that she could retain the air of impersonal indifference that she knew she should be displaying at this time.

Only it was impossible to do so. Impossible to do anything but feel the extraordinary visceral impact on her that he was having.

An impact that suddenly increased exponentially.

He was smiling—and the smile was like the smile of a desert wolf.

Fran felt her lungs squeeze, her breath catch. The smile was swift—a sudden indentation of the firm mouth, a brief flash of teeth, a lightening of his tough features as if the sun had just come out and then disappeared again.

'Forgive me for sounding clichéd, but you don't look the least like an astrophysicist!'

Amusement played around his firm mouth, as if he knew perfectly well that it was, indeed, a clichéd observation, but didn't give a damn. Because the light in those blue, blue eyes of his was telling her just why he'd said what he had.

He wanted to do anything to keep the conversation going.

Fran lifted an eyebrow. Whatever was going on here, it was unlikely to be anything to do with the man's role as a member of the hotel's security team, if that was who he was, given the air of toughness radiating from him. And if he wasn't—if he was just another guest—then that made it no better. He was still chatting her up. So maybe she should just call time and walk.

Except that she didn't want to. The sudden fizzing in her veins, the catch in her heart rate, was telling her that she was reacting to this man as she had never reacted to any man before—that something was happening to her that had never happened to her before.

So, instead of whatever she might have been planning to reply to him with, she could hear her own voice, with a clear hint of answering amusement in it, saying, 'And you've encountered many astrophysicists in your time, have you?'

She was conscious that her eyebrow had lifted, just as her mouth had twitched in amusement, conscious too of how that flashing smile had come again. Her sense was that here was a man totally at ease with himself. Even if he was a security guy, chatting up one of the guests in the hotel he worked in, he didn't care—and he was inviting her not to care either. He was a man who knew he was blatantly accosting a woman who had caught his eye...

She was conscious that long, dark lashes had swept down over those brilliant blue eyes as he answered her in turn.

'Enough,' he said laconically.

Fran's eyes narrowed deliberately. 'Name three,' she challenged.

He laughed—a low, attractive sound that went with the flashing smile, and the brilliant blue eyes and the tough face and the tougher body. All of which were doing incredible things to her.

She felt herself reel inwardly.

What is happening to me? I get chatted up by some guy strolling up to me in a bar at a casino hotel and suddenly I feel like I'm eighteen again. Not a sober-minded post-doc on the far side of twenty-five, who writes abstruse scientific papers on cosmology at a prestigious West Coast university.

Hard-working research academics didn't go doolally because some muscled hunk smiled at them. And nor, came the even more sobering thought, did the woman who was her identity as well as Dr Fran Ristori.

Donna Francesca di Ristori. Offspring of two noble houses—one Italian, one English—both centuries old, with bloodlines that could be traced back to the Middle Ages, and estates and lands, castles and *palazzos*. She was the daughter of Il Marchese d'Arromento, and granddaughter of one of the peers of the British realm, the Duke of Revinscourt.

Not that anyone here in the USA knew that—or cared. In academia only the quality of your research counted, nothing else. It was something that her mother—born Lady Emma, now Marchesa d'Arromento—had never really understood. But then her mother had never really understood why Fran had turned away from the life she'd been born to in order to follow her deep love of learning to the halls of academia.

It had caused, Fran knew, something of a rift between them, and it was only because Fran had agreed to marry into the Italian aristocracy that her mother had been reconciled to her research career.

But last year Fran had broken up with Cesare, Il Conte di Mantegna, whom she had long been expected to marry, and now her mother was barely speaking to her.

'But he was *perfect* for you!' her mother had cried protestingly. 'You've known each other all your lives and he would have let you continue with all this star-gazing you insist on as well as being his Contessa!'

'I got a better offer,' was all Fran had been able to say.

It had been an offer her mother could never have appreciated—the exciting invitation to join the research team of a Nobel Laureate out in California.

Fran had been relieved to take the offer, and not just for herself. Cesare was a friend—a good friend—and he would always be a friend, but it had turned out that he was actually in love with someone else and had since married her.

Fran was glad for Cesare, and for Carla, his new bride, and the baby that had been born to them, and wished them every happiness.

She had moved out to the West Coast, rented an apartment, and was revelling in the heady atmosphere of one of the world's most advanced cosmology research centres. Although it was strange not to have Cesare in her life any longer—even long-distance, across the Atlantic—she had joyfully immersed herself in her work, thrilled to be assisting the famous Nobel Laureate.

Except that this last semester her revered professor had suffered a heart attack and retired prematurely, and his successor wasn't a patch on him. Already Fran had resolved to seek another post, another university. She would see out this conference and then start actively looking.

'OK—I fold.' The man blatantly chatting her up held up a large, square-palmed hand to indicate defeat. 'You called my bluff.'

The flashing smile came again, and yet again Fran felt her heart give a kick. Tomorrow's plenary session, the poster session she was giving—both vanished.

She gave a laugh. She couldn't help it. The guy was so sure of himself. Usually that put her right off, but somehow, in this man, it was simply one more part of his appeal. As to *why* he had that appeal to her—she just could not analyse that. It was beyond rational thought.

'Well, we had the conference dinner tonight, so we're all togged up in our best bib and tucker,' she answered him. 'None of us are looking like nerdy scientists right now!'

Blue, blue eyes swept over her. Open in their admiration for her.

'*Sicuramente no.*' Definitely not.

The murmured syllables were audible, and Fran's expression changed automatically. He wasn't Hispanic after all...

'*Sei Italiano?*'

The question came from her before she could stop himself. The man's expression changed as she asked it. Slight surprise and then clear satisfaction.

Fran realised she'd just given him a whole new avenue to chat her up with. And she found she didn't mind at all.

She didn't notice the slight flicker in his expression as he answered her, nor the very slight air of evasion in his voice.

'Many Americans are,' he said, speaking English now. *'E sei?'* And you?

'Italian on my father's side. English on my mother's,' answered Fran.

With every passing exchange she could feel herself simply giving in to this—whatever it was—and still not really knowing *why* it was happening. Why she should be giving the time of day—make that the time of nearly midnight!—to a muscled hunk who was blazingly sure of himself, blatantly chatting her up, when she really ought to be heading back to her room to go through her presentation for tomorrow.

She only knew a sense of heady breathlessness that had come from nowhere the moment he'd spoken to her. Knew that he was suddenly making her feel so, so different from the sober-minded research academic she knew herself to be—so, so different from the stately Donna Francesca she had been born to be.

He was speaking again. 'English, huh? I thought you were from the East Coast.'

'I lived there for a while,' she allowed. 'Studying for my doctorate.'

A sudden whoop coming from the direction of the post-grads gathered at one of the blackjack tables distracted her and she glanced towards them.

She frowned suddenly. 'I hope they're not trying to beat the dealer by counting in cahoots!' she exclaimed. 'They're all maths hotshots, so they probably could if they tried, but I know casinos don't like that...'

'Don't worry—the croupiers know not to let that happen.'

The words were reassuring, the tone laconic, but Fran glanced at him all the same.

'You sound like you *know* that,' she said.

He nodded, the blue eyes on her. 'I do,' he answered.

She looked at him. So that sounded as if he

was definitely part of hotel security, didn't it? But she still wasn't sure.

Then she realised she didn't care either way. He was speaking again, in that deep, laconic and oh-so-attractive voice of his.

'So, has it been a good conference for you?' he was asking.

She nodded. He was keeping her in conversation. She knew he was, he knew she knew he was, and she was OK with it. She didn't know *why* she was OK with it, but she was. And right now she would give him an answer to his question.

'Yes—it's been mentally stimulating. Full-on, but good. And this hotel…' she gestured with her hand '…is fantastic. I don't really know the Falcone chain, but they've pulled out the stops here. My only regret is that I haven't made enough use of the facilities—I haven't even had a chance to try out the pool. I definitely will tomorrow, though, before we leave. It's just a shame I won't have time to take any of the tours on offer—not even the one to the Grand Canyon!'

The minute she'd said that she regretted it.

Oh, Lord, did he think she was angling for an invitation? She hoped not.

To her relief he let it pass and simply said, 'I'm glad you like the hotel—a lot of work went into it.'

There was professional pride in his voice—she could hear it. It confirmed to her that he must, indeed, be part of the security team that any hotel—let alone one that included a casino—would surely need.

'I'd prefer it without the casino, but there you go. When in Nevada...' she finished insouciantly.

'Casinos make a lot of money,' came the laconic reply, and there was another sweep of those long dark lashes over those blue, blue eyes.

Another whoop of triumph came from the post-grads at the blackjack table.

Fran laughed. 'Maybe a little less tonight,' she observed dryly.

'Maybe,' he allowed, with a glint of amusement in his face, his eyes, around his mouth.

The amusement didn't leave his face, but suddenly there was something else there in his expression—a question. A question that told her, with a quiver of reassurance, that maybe he was not so absolutely sure of himself as he was giving out. And she liked him the more for it.

'And maybe…' he went on, and there was a speculative look in his eyes now that went with the question, that went with the sense that he was in no way taking her answer for granted. 'Maybe,' he continued, the change in his tone of voice matching the change in his expression, 'if I asked if I might buy you a drink to celebrate your fellow astrophysicists' obvious win over there, you might say yes?'

Fran looked at him, glanced back over towards the blackjack table, then looked back at the man who had been chatting her up and was now clearly intent on getting to second base.

Should she co-operate? Did she want to? Or should she say no politely and head to her room to mug up on her presentation?

Even as she cogitated, in the milliseconds it took for her brain's synapses to flash their signals to each other, she felt another emotion stab through her. A sense of restlessness, of wanting something more than to give a fluent presentation the next day. Something more than the hard year of non-stop slog she'd put in since breaking up with Cesare, taking up her research post with the world-famous Nobel Laureate, producing a clutch of published papers with him and his team.

Whoever this blue-eyed, tough-faced, muscled hunk was, and why it was that, for reasons she could not yet figure out, he was capable of drawing her into conversation the way he so effortlessly had, only one thought was dominating her consciousness right now.

No, she didn't want to retire meekly to her room. She wanted, instead, to keep this conversation going, keep this encounter going—keep the rush of fizzing blood in her veins from falling flat.

A smile parted her lips and she climbed back on to the high bar stool. He let her this time, without trying to help. She looked straight at him. Liking what she saw. Going for broke.

'Why not?' she said.

Nic's gaze swept over her with distinct appreciation as she resettled herself on the bar stool. And with gratification too. He hadn't been entirely sure she would accept his move on her.

But that, he knew, was part of her appeal. He was bored with women being over-keen on him, and maybe that was why he was being evasive about who he was—Nicolo Falcone, billionaire founder and owner of the Falcone hotel chain.

For that very reason he threw a warning glance at the barman as he glided up to them, and received an infinitesimal nod of acknowledgement in return.

They gave their orders—a Campari and soda for her, a bourbon for him—and Nic lowered himself to sit beside her on the next bar stool.

'So,' he opened, 'are you giving any papers yourself at the conference?'

'Yes, a post—that's a small presentation— about where I've got to in my current research. It's for tomorrow, before the final plenary session.'

'What's it about—and would I even understand the title?' he added with good-humoured self-deprecation.

For all that her incandescent beauty lit up the room for him, she lived in a world that was far, far distant from the cut and thrust of his.

He watched her take a sip from her drink, admiring her delicate fingers, the elegant air she had about her. She was wearing a mid-price-range cocktail dress, with a square neckline and cap sleeves, which, although it was fitting for the purpose of a formal conference dinner, had little pizzazz about it. Her hair was dressed in a neat pleat, and her make-up was subdued. She looked what she was—an academic dressed up for the evening.

Desire curled in him, focussed and demanding.

She was answering him now, and he paid attention, subduing his primitive response to her.

Her voice, light and crisp in the English style, had warmed with an enthusiasm that came, he knew instinctively, from the intellectual passion in her that lit up in her eyes, animating her fine-boned face.

'My research field is cosmology—understanding the origins and eventual fate of the universe. This poster is just one small aspect of that. I'm running observational data through a computer model, testing various options for the geometry and density of space which might indicate whether, to put it at its simplest, the universe is open or closed.'

Nic frowned in concentration. 'What does that mean?'

Her voice warmed yet more as she explained. 'Well, if it's open, the expansion that started with the Big Bang will cause all the matter in the universe to be dissipated, so there will be no stars, no planets, no galaxies and no energy. It's called heat death and it would be really boring,' she said with a moue of dislike. 'So I'm rooting for a closed universe, which could cause everything to eventually collapse back in a Big Crunch and trigger another Big Bang—and the universe will be reborn. Far more fun!'

Nic took a mouthful of bourbon, feeling the strong liquid ease pleasantly down his throat.

'So, which is it?' he asked in his laconic fashion.

She gave another moue. 'No one knows for sure—though it's tending towards open at the moment, alas. Whichever it is we have to accept it—even if I don't like it.'

Nic felt himself shake his head. 'No. I don't buy that.'

She was looking at him questioningly, her eyes beautiful and wide.

He elaborated, his voice decisive. 'We should never accept what we don't like. It's defeatist.' His jaw set. 'OK, maybe it applies to the universe—but it doesn't apply to humanity. We can change things, and it's up to us. We don't have to accept the status quo.'

She was still looking at him, but her expression was one of curiosity now. 'That sounds like it runs very deep in you,' she said. Her eyes rested on him a moment, as if reading him.

He gave a half-shrug of one shoulder, as if impatient. 'We can't just accept things as they are.'

She frowned slightly. 'Some things we have to, though. Some things we can't change. Who we are, for example. Who we were born as—'

Like I was born Donna Francesca—that's in me whether I want it to be or not. It's part of my heritage—an indelible part. For all the changes I've made to my life, I can't change my birth.

'That's *exactly* what we can change!' There was vehemence in his reply, and he took another slug of bourbon. Memories were pressing in on him suddenly—*bad* memories. His hapless mother, abandoned by the man who'd fathered her son, abandoned by all of the other men who'd taken up with her—or worse. His memory darkened. Like the brute who had inflicted beatings on her until the day had come when Nic had reached his teenage years and had been strong enough to protect her from thugs like that....

I had to change my life! I had to do it for myself—by myself. There was no one to help me. And I did *change it.*

She was looking at him, a slightly curious look in her eyes at the vehemence of his expression, her beautiful grey eyes clear in her fine-boned face.

She gave a slow nod. 'Then perhaps,' she said, in an equally slow voice, 'we have to bear in mind that old prayer, don't we? The one that asks that we be granted the courage to change what we can, but the patience to accept what we can't, and the wisdom to know the difference.'

Nic thought about it. Then, 'Nope,' he said decisively. 'I want to change everything I don't like.'

She gave a laugh—a deliberately light one.

'Well, you wouldn't make a scientist, that's for sure,' she said.

He gave an echoing laugh, realising with a sense of shock that he had spoken more about his deepest feelings to this woman than he had ever done to anyone. It struck him that to have touched on matters that ran so very deep within him with a woman he hadn't known existed twenty minutes earlier was....

Significant?

I don't have conversations like this with women—never. So why this one?

It had to be because of her being a scientist—that had to be it. It was just that, nothing more.

She's a fantastically beautiful woman—and I want to know her more. But there have been a lot of beautiful women in my life, when I've had time for them. She's just one more.

She was different, yes, because of her being an incredibly talented astrophysicist when the women he was usually interested in were party girls, prioritising good times and carefree enjoyment, which allowed him time out from his obsession with building his personal empire. Females who didn't ask for commitment. For more than he could give them.

But thinking about the assorted women who'd been and gone in his life was not what he was here to do. He was here to make the most of this one.

He flexed his shoulders, feeling himself relax again, his eyes focussed on drinking in her extraordinary entrancing beauty.

She had finished her drink, and so had he. With every instinct in his body, long honed by experience, he knew it was time to call time on the evening. He'd set the wheels in motion, but tonight was not going to get them further to the destination he wanted for them both. She was not, he knew, the kind of woman who could be rushed. He'd followed through on the impulse that had brought him across the casino floor to her, and for now that was enough.

He signalled the barman, signed the chit as presented, making sure his scrawling *'Falcone'* was visible only to his employee, and got to his feet with a smile.

Fran did likewise. Her emotions were strange—new to her—but she smiled politely. 'Thank you for the drink,' she said.

The long dark lashes swept over the blue, blue eyes. 'My pleasure,' came the laconic reply. 'And thank you for the science tutorial,' he added, the smile warm in his gaze.

'You're welcome,' Fran replied, her smile just as warm, but briefer, more circumspect.

She headed towards the bank of elevators across the lobby, conscious of his gaze upon her. Was she regretting the fact that he was calling time on their encounter? Surely not? Surely anything more was out of the question?

And yet even as with her head she knew it must be, with quite a different part of her body she knew—from the heady buzz in her bloodstream and the quickened heart rate—that she was regretful that she must retire to her solitary bedroom.

That sense of restlessness she'd felt earlier filled her again. Cesare had been a long time ago—over a year ago now—and anyway, theirs had never been a physical relationship. That, she knew, would have waited until well into their engagement, or even their actual wedding night, for Cesare was a traditionally-minded Italian male.

Not many would have understood their relationship—understood that, having known each other all their lives, it had made perfect sense for them to marry one day. In the meantime, they had both been single agents, and she was well aware that Cesare—an extremely attractive male, blessed with a high social position and great wealth to boot—had indulged in many a romantic liaison.

He had accepted that such tolerance was two-way, and until they had become formally engaged she had been as free as he to indulge in affairs. She'd had only two what might be called 'full affairs' in her life—one with another undergrad at Cambridge, a very boy-girl romance, and one brief liaison with a visiting academic while on her PhD course on the East Coast—and that had amply sufficed.

Her dating had nearly always been with fellow academics, and usually based around concerts, films or theatre outings. Searing passion had not played a role, and its absence had not troubled her. One day, after all, she would be marrying Cesare...

Except that now she wouldn't, after all.

She was footloose and fancy-free. If she chose to be. Free to move on from Cesare, to seek romance—free to take a break, if she wanted, from the demands of academia.

Free to be chatted up by a muscled hunk with the bluest eyes she'd ever seen in a man, let alone one of Italian origin. A man whose smile was lazy, his speech laconic, and whose expression and long-lashed deep blue eyes were telling her just how very much he appreciated her.

She jabbed at the elevator button, her feeling of restlessness increasing as she stepped inside, feeling it swoop her the couple of floors upwards in this low-rise hotel that blended so gracefully into the desert landscape.

Inside her room, she glanced at the folder with her notes, but did not open it. Instead she stripped off for bed, taking off her make-up, brushing out her hair. Wondering why her heart rate still was not back to normal.

Her dreams, when they came, were full—and unsettling.

CHAPTER TWO

THE CONFERENCE WAS wrapping up, with the panel of plenary speakers paying courteous tribute to each other.

Fran flexed her tired fingers, having taken copious notes throughout. Her thoughts were uncertain. She was scheduled to fly back to the West Coast with her colleagues that afternoon, but was conscious that she was reluctant to do so. She'd meant what she'd said about wanting to take advantage of the hotel's amenities, and why shouldn't she? She hadn't taken any holiday time for a year—she was overdue for a break. So why not here and now?

And whether that hunky security guy chatting her up last night had anything to do with her decision, she would not consider. He'd been a catalyst for it, that was all.

The sense of restlessness that had started to well up in her again subsided, her decision made. She said as much to her colleagues, telling them that she would be staying on for a few days at the hotel.

Grinning, they informed her they were off to hit Vegas and see if their luck at the tables was holding out. Fran wished them well and waved them off. Las Vegas was one place she did *not* want to go to.

No, if she went anywhere it would be to see something of the western desert—maybe even, she pondered, as she headed for the reception desk to keep her room on, take one of the hotel's tours to the Grand Canyon.

She made enquiries, took away the tour brochure, and headed into the poolside bistro to have a light lunch and go through her notes. Her mind felt wiped out from all the heavy-duty presentations, and she realised she was looking forward to a few days off.

As she tucked into her salad she found herself wondering if she would see that hunky security guy again. But if he'd been on duty the night before maybe he wasn't around in the daytime? Or if he was maybe he wouldn't show any further interest in her anyway? Or maybe—

'Hi—so, conference all finished?'

The deep, gravelled voice sounded behind her, and Fran turned her head. Felt something quiver inside her as she set her eyes on his powerful body again. This time he was not in a tux, but in a dark burgundy polo shirt bearing the hotel's logo—the words Falcone, Nevada, with a golden falcon, wings outstretched, above—that stretched across his broad, muscled chest in a way that made her want to study the contours minutely.

That internal quiver came again, and a quickening of her heart rate. She felt something lift inside her…a sense of lightness.

'All done,' she acknowledged. 'Just the notes to go through.' She gestured at the pile of papers in the folder.

He glanced at them, and then at her. 'May I?' He indicated the free seat at her table.

He was asking her—courteously—if he could continue their slight acquaintance. Fran saw it and registered the courtesy, the request.

She knew she was entirely free to say something like, *Oh, I'm sorry, but I really do need to go through my notes straight away while they're fresh in my head*, and he would simply accept it, give her a regretful smile and stroll away. Accept her rejection.

But those words of polite rejection never came. Instead she heard her voice say, just as courteously, 'Of course,' and she smiled.

She felt that lift again inside her—in her body, in her spirits. Seeing him again was reinforcing the extraordinary reaction she'd had to him last night—confirming it for her. Whatever was going on, something different was happening to her.

And she would let it happen. Mentally, the decision had been made. And as he lowered his powerful frame on to the chair, with a grace and ease that she found pleasing to the eye, she knew she would let him continue with his move on her.

For a move it was—that was obvious. Inexperienced she might be, compared with many of her contemporaries, but she knew when a man was making a play for her. And this one was. Quite decidedly.

So his next words came as no surprise.

'You've decided not to check out yet—I'm glad.'

She threw him an old-fashioned look. Clearly

he'd had a word with the staff at the reception desk, discovered she'd extended her booking.

Nic returned her look with a bland expression. He was deliberately wearing the staff polo shirt today, to confirm the impression he guessed she had that he was one of his own employees. That suited him fine.

'Glad?' she queried. *Challenged.*

The bland expression did not falter. 'Glad you'll have a chance to enjoy the hotel's leisure amenities—and maybe take one of the tours as well?'

His glance now went to the hotel tour brochure. It was extensive—part of the offering the resort made to visitors. It included personalised tours to anywhere in the US West they might want to visit. Far or near.

'Maybe,' he went on, his expression still bland, but belied by a glint in those incredibly blue dark-lashed eyes that was telling Fran something not bland in the slightest, 'you might like to start with the Sunset Drive this evening?'

Fran's heart gave a little unconscious skip but she frowned slightly—her first glance at the brochure hadn't listed such a tour.

'It's one of the personalised ones.' On cue came the answer to her unspoken question. His voice was as bland as his expression. 'It sets off from here late afternoon, going to a viewing spot for the sunset. It's only a couple of hours. You'll be back in time for dinner.'

He smiled. Not the desert wolf smile, but a bland smile, his long dark lashes dipping over his blue, blue eyes.

Fran considered it. Carefully analysed it for all the pros and cons for all of five seconds. Then gave her answer.

'Sounds good,' she said, and smiled a bland smile in return.

'Great,' he said.

Satisfaction was in his voice. Mission accomplished. Fran heard it, and it amused her. Nothing about this man was putting her off. He was being open about his intentions—conspiratorial, even. And yet she realised she still didn't actually know whether this Sunset Drive was really part of the hotel's offering to guests or was a particularly personalised tour, customised for herself alone.

That he would turn out to be the driver for

this Sunset Drive, and she the sole passenger, she had little doubt at all.

And no reservations either.

He got to his feet—again, remarkably smoothly and easily for a man with his powerful frame—and smiled down at her again. His expression was just a touch less bland. A touch more openly appreciative.

'I'll fix it,' he said, and lifted a hand in casual farewell and strolled away.

As he went Fran's eyes went after him, saw how he paused to say something to one of the waitresses—a young woman whose expression as he talked to her told Fran that she was not the only female susceptible to that unforced, laid-back charm, those powerful good looks. Whatever the man had to draw women to him he had it in spades.

She gave a little sigh that turned into a good-humoured wry smile. She'd felt restless, mentally wiped from the conference—as if she were surfacing after a long, intensely focussed cerebral engagement that had lasted a whole year since she'd realised that making her life with Cesare was not what she wanted to do after all.

And now suddenly, out of nowhere, the future was beckoning to her. A future that was her own—that held more than her career. That held adventure—

And if that adventure, for now, happened to include a man who was making it very clear that she was pleasing to his eye—a man who was pleasing *her* eye in a way that was as totally unexpected as it was unpredicted—well, she would go for that.

She felt that lift inside her come again, that heady quickening of her pulse.

And welcomed it.

'Hi, let me help you up.'

Nic handed Fran up into the SUV he'd commandeered and parked on the hotel forecourt, before vaulting into the driver's seat. He'd changed into a western shirt, jeans and boots, and saw that for her part she'd sensibly put on firmer footwear, a loose shirt and long cotton trousers.

'One Sunset Drive coming up,' he said, casting his wolf-like smile at her, making Fran glad she was wearing sunglasses. Making her glad she was taking a chance for a change.

He fired the engine, easing the SUV down the hotel drive on to the main highway, then turning to her as he settled into a cruising speed. 'So, did you enjoy your leisurely afternoon, Dr Ristori?'

It was an amiable, courteous enquiry, and she answered in kind, accepting that he must know her name from the hotel register. 'Yes, I wrote up my notes then got in a swim and flopped on a lounger poolside. Totally lazy.'

'Well, why not?' he answered easily. 'Your vacation—your choice.'

He glanced at her—a throwaway glance that was hidden by his aviator sunglasses, accompanied by a smile indenting around his mouth. It was a friendly, open smile, yet one that acknowledged that behind the word 'choice' there was more than whether or not she had had a lazy afternoon.

A lot more might be hers to choose.

She answered with a flickering smile and looked away, down the dusty road stretching through the desert landscape like something out of a Western movie.

He didn't talk any more as he drove, and after

some miles he turned off up an unmade track, along the edge of a bluff that terminated in a rocky col overlooking a valley beyond, where he parked.

As they got out the heat and the silence enveloped them. Nic jammed a wide-brimmed hat on his head, offering her one for herself, which she dutifully donned against the glare of the lowering sun. He then helped himself to a backpack holding twin water bottles and the mandatory emergency kit.

'It's about a ten-minute hike now,' Nic said, and set off up a trail that led higher among the rugged outcrops.

Fran followed nimbly, and as they gained height saw the valley beyond fill with deep golden light, the azure sky arching above. It seemed very far from anywhere, with only the wind keening in her ears. Eventually they reached a flat outcrop affording a ringside view of the sight they had come to see and they settled down, backs against the warm rock behind them.

'Now we wait,' Nic said.

He passed her a water bottle and Fran drank

thirstily. So did he. Before their eyes the sun was starting to lower into the horizon, turning deep bronze as it did so. Fran gazed, mesmerised, glad of her sunglasses as the sun seemed to fuse with the earth, flushing the azure sky with a halo of deep crimson until finally it slipped beyond the rim of the ever-turning globe and the sky began to darken.

She slid the dark glasses from her face, and saw him do likewise. Then he turned to her.

'Worth it?' he asked laconically.

She nodded. 'Oh, yes,' she breathed.

Her eyes met his, held, and for a moment—just a moment—something was exchanged between them. Something that seemed to go with this slow, unhurried landscape, desolate but with a beauty of its own, lonely but intensely special.

A thought occurred to her, and she heard herself give voice to it.

'I don't know your name,' she said. She said it with a little frown, as if it were strange to have shared this moment with him not knowing it.

He gave her his slow smile, holding out his strong, large hand.

'Nic,' he said. 'Nic Rossi.'

He gave his birth name quite deliberately. He didn't want complications—he wanted things to be very, very simple.

She took his hand, felt its strength and warmth. Felt more than its strength and warmth.

'Fran,' she said. Her smile met his. Her eyes met his. Acknowledging something that needed to be acknowledged between them. The fact that, whatever was going on, from this moment she was no longer a hotel guest and he was not part of the security team, or whatever his role was.

That this was something between them— only between them.

'Doc Fran,' Nic murmured contemplatively, his eyes working over her. He nodded. 'It suits you.'

He didn't release her hand, only drew her upright as he climbed to his feet as well.

'We need to head down before the light goes,' he told her, and carefully they made their way back to the SUV. 'Hungry?' Nic asked. He kept his question studiedly casual. 'Because if you don't want to head back to the hotel yet I know a diner nearby...'

He let the suggestion hang, let her choose to answer it as she wanted.

She gave her flickering smile—the one that told him she was hovering between holding back and not holding back.

'That sounds good,' she answered. 'A change from the hotel.'

He gunned the engine and they headed off, headlights cutting through the desert dusk that had turned to night by the time they drew up in the car park of a roadside diner.

It was a typical western diner, with a friendly, laid-back atmosphere and staff in the customary western outfits that went with the setting.

They ate at a table overlooking the desert, making themselves comfortable on the padded banquettes. Fran stuck to iced tea, but Nic had a beer, and they both ordered steak.

Hers was so massive she cut off a third, placing it on Nic's plate. 'You need to feed your muscles,' she told him with a smile, refusing to let herself think that it was a strangely intimate gesture.

He laughed. 'I'll trade you my salad,' he said, and pushed the bowl towards her.

'Salad's good for you!' she protested, and pushed it back.

His hand was still on the bowl. Did her fingers brush against his hand? She didn't know. Knew only that she pulled her hand away and that as she did so she felt it tingle, as though, maybe, she had made contact. Electrical contact...

She started to eat her steak. Made some remark about its tenderness. Any remark.

What am I doing?

The question framed itself. Rhetorical. Unnecessary. She knew what she was doing—knew perfectly well.

I'm on a date. Not official. Not announced. Not planned. But a date, all the same. We've watched the sun go down together, and now we're eating together.

And what would they do next together?

She didn't answer that one. Didn't want to. Not yet. Not now.

Instead she asked a question—something about the desert. After all, he worked in this region—he must know more about it than she did. And, whatever Italian-American locality he came from originally, right now he was way more a native here than she was.

He answered the question readily, and all her other questions, but sometimes he shrugged and said he didn't know. So they asked the diners at another table, obviously locals, who assumed they were tourists.

Fran did not enlighten them.

They also assumed they were a couple.

Fran did not enlighten them on that either.

Supposing we were.

The thought was in her head. Tantalising. Making her wonder. Speculate. Was that why she was sharing dinner with him now? Because she was accepting that she was willing to take things further between them?

But just how far?

She felt her mind thinking ahead. An affair? No, maybe not even that. A—a fling. That was more like it. Something out of the ordinary in her life…something that wouldn't happen twice—because he was from a world different from her, as she was from him.

But that doesn't matter.

Her eyes went to his face again, slid down over his strong, muscled body. The flicker of electricity came again—a kind of current flowing between them, strengthening, or so it seemed to her, with every circuit that it made. She didn't know why…knew only that it was powerful and enticing.

Why not? Why not take this opportunity if it comes? I need to move on from Cesare. I need something…different. It would be good for me—mark a new chapter in my life.

Would Nic Rossi—so entirely different from any man she'd known before, so rawly, powerfully attractive to her—be it?

The question circled in her head. They'd finished eating—steaks demolished, side orders too—and now Nic was leaning back in his chair, letting his weight tilt it back, easing his broad shoulders. Relaxed, leonine, powerful.

Sexy as hell.

The phrase forced its way into her head. It was not one she'd ever used about a man. Not a phrase that had fitted any man she'd ever known. Not even Cesare. Her lips twisted. Cesare would have loathed any woman calling him that. Nic, she suspected, with another twist of her lips, but this time with humour in it, would simply take it as his due.

He knows he can pull. It's in him, in every cell of his body. It's part of him. It isn't arrogance or conceit—it's just... Well, it just is, that's all. And he'd be glad I'm thinking it.

She didn't need to spell it out. Didn't need to think about it. Didn't need to analyse it or wonder about it or speculate about it. All she needed to do right now was answer the question he was asking her as he picked up the menu, flicked it over to the dessert list.

'Ice cream?' he asked.

Fran smiled. That was one decision that was easy to make.

'Oh, yes,' she said. 'Definitely.'

They drove back to the hotel, the moon rising to the east, the night ablaze with stars. Nic had seen Fran glance upwards as they got back into the SUV and an idea had struck him. As they drove he gave voice to it.

'Would you have any interest,' he opened, glancing at her briefly, then back to the ink-dark road, 'in maybe taking off to see the South-West Array tomorrow?'

She turned her head. 'Could we do it in a day?' she asked. Unconsciously, she had used the word 'we', and it registered a moment later. But she didn't mind that she had. It seemed right that she had.

'If we make an early start,' Nic said. He paused. 'So, how about it?'

'Oh, yes!' Fran answered, enthusiasm in her voice. 'You know,' she mused, 'as a theoretical physicist I simply use the data that the observational physicists provide for me, to test my theories—but to actually see *where* they get that data is always a privilege. The South-West Array is only just coming on-stream—'

She fished in her bag for her phone, looked it up. Her face brightened.

'Nic, *could* we? I can message them tonight, see if I can get in touch with one of the onsite guys tomorrow...' She paused. 'It might be boring for you, though,' she warned.

Then she wondered whether she should have said that. Maybe this was just another tour laid on by the hotel, with her own personal chauffeur? But she didn't think that—not now. Not any longer. Not after sharing steak and ice-cream at a roadside diner.

This isn't about his job, or even mine. This is about us.

She felt the now familiar skip of her heart rate, telling her she was glad—glad that that was what it was about. Then she realised Nic was speaking again.

'You can give me another physics tutorial on the way there,' he said. 'The elementary version, that is.'

There was a smile in his voice, and in hers as she answered. 'Physics is usually simple—it's just the maths that's hard!'

He laughed, that low, gravelly sound that she was getting used to sending a little frisson through her—a frisson that she felt again as, gaining the hotel's rear car park, he helped her step down, retaining her hand just a fraction longer than was necessary. Then he was opening a side door and they were heading down a deserted corridor towards the lobby.

As they did, a service door opened and someone emerged. He glanced at Nic as they headed past.

'Evening, boss.'

Nic acknowledged him with a brief nod, and as the staff member passed by, Fran murmured, 'Boss?'

'He's on my team,' Nic answered smoothly.

They arrived at the elevators. Nic was glad that no other members of his staff were around, and without waiting to be invited he stepped inside the lift with her.

'I'll see you to your room,' he said.

Fran made no demur, but suddenly, out of nowhere, she was supremely conscious of the confined space of the elevator, of Nic's closeness to her, of her own heightened sense of the moment. Would he try and kiss her? She tensed, not knowing whether she wanted him to or not.

He made no move on her, however, just waited until she had opened her room door and was turning to bid him goodnight, finding it hard to take her eyes from him when she was this close to him.

His hand splayed against the doorjamb, enclosing her. 'Thank you for tonight,' he said. 'It's been good.'

There was a low note in his voice, a huskiness, and a smile— she could hear it, see the slight curve of his mouth, the dip of his long, long lashes over those blue, blue eyes. And then, while she was still gazing up at him, his mouth was lowering to hers.

It was a kiss like none she'd known. Slow, deliberate, and for one purpose only. To tell her what she could have if she chose to.

She gave herself to it, her eyelids fluttering closed, feeling her shoulders sag against the door, her hands slacken as her whole being became focussed on the sensation he was drawing from her.

It was like a kind of silken velvet, moving over her leisurely, tasting, exploring, taking his time. And then, without her even realising, he was deepening the kiss, easing her lips apart. Letting her taste, enjoy his tasting, enjoy what there was between them. What more there could be.

She felt arousal flare within her, more powerful than she had ever felt, more intense, more sensuous, and she yielded her willing mouth to his, feeling the pleasure of it until, it seemed like an age later, he was drawing back from her, gliding his mouth over her, skimming leisurely over her parted lips, a velvet withdrawal.

He lifted his head and her eyes fluttered open, looked into his gaze. So close…so very close to hers. She felt dazed, dizzy. He smiled, seeing her reaction to his kiss, liking it.

He stepped away, giving her a little space. 'Goodnight, Doc Fran,' he said, but there was intimacy in the way he said it. 'Sleep well.'

She gave a reply, and then he was turning away, heading back down the corridor. She watched him reach the elevators. Felt dizziness inside her still.

Knew that whatever this man wanted of her she wanted it too.

Nic did not sleep well that night in the suite he'd reserved for himself at this, his latest multi-million-dollar acquisition. He lay sleepless, gazing at the shadowed ceiling, one arm crooked behind his head, feeling a mix of restlessness, satisfaction and anticipation.

Dio, but how he'd wanted to stay with her! That kiss had been like dipping his finger into a pot of honey to taste the sweetness, and it had told him she had found it just as pleasurable as he had. But it had also told him, just as every instinct since he'd first set eyes on her had told him, that she was not a woman to be hurried. She was no hedonistic party girl. She was a mature, highly intelligent woman, who would make her decision in her own time, in her own way, about indulging in a romance with him.

And if she did, as he burningly hoped she would, it would not be conducted here at the hotel. He liked it that to her he was not Nicolo Falcone, and if they stayed here it was bound to come out at some point. That encounter in the corridor had been a warning of that inevitability. No, better that they took off to somewhere he was not known, so that he was still simply Nic Rossi to her.

Nic Rossi—his birth name, abandoned so long ago, when he'd first set out to forge his glittering empire, echoed in his mind. It had been strange to use it again. As strange as remembering the way he'd revealed so much of his own deep feelings and his passionate beliefs to her in that very first conversation he'd had with her the previous night. His belief never to accept what life had dumped you with—to make someone new of yourself by effort and dedication and determination.

His thoughts moved on. Back to the familiar territory of his empire-building. He ran through his latest ambitions to launch a flagship hotel in Manhattan. It wouldn't be easy, let alone cheap to achieve, but he'd do it in the end. He always did. Always. The determination to succeed in business never left him.

And to succeed on more pleasurable fronts too.

His thoughts went back to the breathtakingly beautiful, entrancing blonde, the oh-so-lovely Doc Fran, alone in her lonely bed—alone for one last night.

He smiled, anticipation filling him again.

'Oh, wow!' Fran breathed, her eyes widening at the sight appearing before them as the SUV gained the low brow of a hill, revealing what was beyond.

It was like something out of a sci-fi film— other-worldly—with a vast matrix of huge dish antennae, angled upwards to catch the faintest radio whisper of distant stars, each one set on rails for moving into precise position.

The whole place was perimeter-fenced, but they drove up to the visitor centre, where Fran identified herself as from her university and promptly got the attention of one of the technical staff to show them around.

Nic was as impressed as anyone would be by

the engineering feats achieved, but understood scarcely a word of their erudite exchanges. He was content just to see how the animation in her face, the interest in her keen, intelligent eyes, only enhanced her beauty, her appeal to him.

As they finally left the array she was fulsome in her thanks. He gave her his slashing smile. 'This morning was your treat—this afternoon is mine. But you'll enjoy it, I promise you.'

She did, too—though she gasped breathlessly as Nic showed her just why it was *his* treat.

They drove on another forty miles or so to a reservoir lake with a water resort, where they lunched at a waterfront café. Then Nic led her out along the jetty and hired the leanest, meanest motorboat available.

And hit the accelerator.

Fran's breath and speech were blown far behind her, her hair streaming, her hands clutching at the rails as the boat flew across the lake, the bow hitting the water's surface as if it was concrete. Italian words broke from her—and she heard Nic laugh, realised he could understand her expletives, and her description of him as a certifiable maniac who would kill them both.

'No way! You're safe as a baby!' he yelled at her, in the same language, his face alight with laughter.

He bombed across the width of the lake, slewing around in a huge arcing curve of water that caught the sun's rays in a million rainbows before racing back towards the jetty again.

Within reach of it he slowed and turned to Fran. Her hair was a wild tangle, her eyes alight with laughter. Nic let his arm slide around her shoulder and pulled her against him.

'Fun?' he asked.

He didn't really have to ask. It was visible in her face.

She let her head rest on his shoulder, feeling it strong beneath her cheek. 'Most fun ever,' she said.

'Happy to please you,' he said, and dropped a kiss on her forehead.

Such a slight gesture, such a slight tightening of his arm around her... They sat beside each other, his other hand on the wheel, guiding the boat lightly on the water as if he were Cesare on one of his thoroughbreds.

Fran's eyes flickered slightly, and she wondered why, of all things, she was thinking of Cesare now.

Nic saw it, saw her expression change. 'What is it?' he asked quietly.

She looked at him, easing away a little, but not freeing herself. 'I'm thinking of the man I nearly married,' she said.

Nic stilled. It was impossible to think of her married, or even engaged—taken by another man. Not when he wanted her himself so much.

'What happened?' he heard his voice asking. He heard the tension in it, but didn't know why it was there.

'I broke it off,' she said. 'I'd just been offered a research post out on the West Coast, working with a Nobel Laureate, and I couldn't resist it. And I was pretty sure,' she added slowly, 'that Cesare was involved with someone else anyway.'

'Then he was nuts,' said Nic bluntly. 'Nuts to prefer someone else to you.'

She gave a little laugh. 'Thank you,' she said. 'But he and I…we never—well, you know. It wasn't an affair that we had. It was a— Well, I guess a kind of *expectation*. We'd known each other all our lives. It would have worked, him and me.'

'Cesare?' mused Nic, registering the Italian name, which she'd pronounced in the Italian way. 'So—back in the old country?'

'Very much so,' she said dryly, thinking of just how sizeable a chunk of 'the old country' Cesare's estates covered.

Nic eased the throttle again. He didn't want to know any more about the guy that she'd nearly married and hadn't. Right now he wanted to be the only male in her vision, her thoughts.

Her desires.

At a much slower pace he nosed the boat forward again, keeping his arm around Fran, where he wanted it to be.

'Let's see what's at the far end of the lake,' he said.

The sun was lowering by the time they handed the boat in. Nic turned to her. Her hair was still windblown, her skin sun-kissed even with sunblock. She looked effortlessly lovely.

'What next?' he asked.

His eyes were light on her, the question in his voice putting the decision in her hands.

The choice of what was to happen—or not—between them now.

Fran's expression flickered. 'It's a long way back to the Falcone,' she observed. 'Maybe too far?' Her glance went to the resort motel that was set back on a low bluff.

'Not in the Falcone league,' Nic said, 'but it looks passable.'

He kept his voice neutral, not wanting to show his satisfaction that she was indicating they should stay there together. As he so wanted.

Fran gave a wry smile. 'There speaks a loyal employee of the famous Falcone chain!' she answered lightly.

Then she nodded, as if making a silent decision for herself. Maybe thinking about Cesare, talking about him, had confirmed her feelings. Told her that whatever it was that was happening between her and Nic, she wanted it to happen.

'OK…' She took a breath. 'Let's go for it.'

Even so, she booked separate rooms at Reception—and not just because anything else might have seemed too…obvious. She definitely needed a bathroom and a bedroom entirely to herself—her wind-tangled hair and water-splashed day-worn clothes were a disaster.

Gratefully spotting a small retail outlet, inset into the lobby, she plunged in.

It was a good hour before she was ready to meet Nic in the motel's bar. As he rose to greet her, she laughed.

'Snap!'

They had both, it seemed, availed themselves of the retail outlet's offerings—and not just shampoo and toiletries for her, and a razor for him. They were both now wearing tee shirts bearing the name of the lake, Fran's in pink and Nic's in blue.

But where Nic was making do with the chinos he'd been wearing all day, Fran had found a wraparound cotton skirt in white seersucker that floated gracefully to mid-calf to replace her water-stained Bermuda shorts. Her newly washed hair tumbled over her shoulders, and her only make-up was a touch of mascara and lip gloss.

She knew Nic's eyes were warm upon her.

But then, hers were warm on him, too. He was cleanly shaven, damp hair feathering at the nape of his neck, and the deep blue tee shirt matched his eyes and lovingly moulded his torso. But he was no muscle-bound Adonis. That innate air of Italian style he possessed was overwhelming—the kind of automatic male display that she was used to seeing in her countrymen. It was not vanity, or showing off, but it came instinctively to them.

'You look *so* Italian,' she heard herself say as they took their happy hour cocktails over to a table looking out across the darkening lake. She studied his face consideringly. 'I wonder where the blue eyes come from? Some Norman ancestor way back...rampaging through the peninsula to make a kingdom for themselves?'

Nic thought about it and liked the idea. He'd made his own kingdom—the Falcone kingdom—deliberately choosing that new name for himself because it made him want to fly high, swoop down on his prey, fly ever higher.

'What about your grey eyes and blonde hair?' he asked in return. 'Are they from your English mother?'

She nodded, not wishing to elaborate about her parentage, aware that she did not want to bring that side of her into what was happening now. Here, with Nic, she was 'Doc Fran'—she smiled inwardly at his amusedly bestowed moniker—and that was all she wanted to be.

The fact that her mother, Lady Emma, would consider it incomprehensible that her daughter might want to take off as she had with someone who worked in hotel security was irrelevant to her. Her whole other identity, as Donna Francesca, was also irrelevant, as it always was when she was here in the USA, whether it was in her university department, or now, here, with Nic.

And Nic was—well, just Nic. And she didn't want him any other way. He had a strength to him, a quality to his character that was as evident as his physical strength. It lay beneath the casual, laid-back attitude—a sure knowledge of his own worth, but without any need to display it. She liked him all the more for it.

He was asking her, now, how she had become an astrophysicist, and she answered readily.

'I fell in love with science at school, because it explained everything about the world. And physics and astronomy just captivated me,' she said. She paused, then heard herself add, 'My family was less enthusiastic.' She frowned, her mouth setting. 'My father came round, because he's always been very indulgent with me, but my mother—'

She broke off. She was saying more than she wanted to. More than she ever said to people, admitted…

'Wanted you to marry and settle down to be a wife and home-maker?' Nic finished for her. The name of the rejected former fiancé hovered in his head but he pushed it aside.

Fran nodded heavily, taking a mouthful of her strawberry daiquiri. 'Yes,' she said briefly.

For all that her home would have been a vast medieval *castello*, and she would have been a *contessa*, Nic had nailed it.

She took a breath. 'Oh, they're proud of me now, but my mother hasn't forgiven me for ditching Cesare—'

She broke off, and Nic did not pick her up on it again. He didn't want her remembering the man she hadn't married.

She was speaking again, and he realised she'd turned the conversation to him. That was something he didn't want either. But it was too late to halt her.

'What about you, Nic? How did you come to be where you are in life now?'

He paused, his tequila mid-way to his mouth. He lowered it again slowly, his eyes veiled.

'Well, it wasn't thanks to my schooldays,' he heard himself saying.

His voice sounded grim. Bleak, even to his own ears.

'What I learnt at school was how not to get beaten up or corralled into running drugs for the gangs.' His mouth tightened and he looked across at Fran. 'I left as soon as I could and went to work. It was a fancy hotel and I was way down in the basement!'

His expression changed now, his eyes clearing.

'But it changed everything for me,' he said. 'I was earning money—not much, but it was my own, through my own efforts. And I could see, for the first time, a future for me. Something I could make for myself, *of* myself. Out of the nothing I'd been handed at birth, despite all the expectations that I'd amount to nothing!'

She heard the vehemence in his voice and it resonated with her—their defiance of what had been expected of them, each in their very different ways.

'What about your parents?' she asked. Her

voice was sympathetic, admiring of the way he'd fought and won his grim battles.

Nic's mouth twisted, and he reached for his tequila, taking a deep draught. 'My father wasn't there—I never knew him. He cleared out before I was born. And my poor mother—'

He broke off again. Took another mouthful of tequila.

'Well, let's just say that she had a bad time with men. The final man landed her in hospital.' His eyes darkened. 'I put *him* in hospital too—and never regretted it!' His expression changed again, the darkness lessening. 'Although she was an invalid she lived long enough to see me make good, and I'll always be grateful for that.'

He took a final slug of his tequila, finishing it and getting to his feet. The air of grim darkness had dropped from him and he wanted it gone. Wanted only to focus on the now. He held his hand out to Fran, the woman he wanted for this very enticing *now*.

'Time to eat,' he announced.

She took the outstretched hand, liking the way he was wanting to join the present again.

She smiled at him as she stood up. 'Sounds good,' she said.

Without conscious realisation she walked with him into the restaurant, not having dropped his hand. His strong fingers closed around hers, warm and reassuring.

The 'now' of their being together seemed very good.

Yet across her consciousness slid the thought that they had exchanged more about themselves, about what drove them, what they'd overcome, in their brief time together than so casual an acquaintance would usually expect.

Maybe, she mused as they took their places at the table in the motel's restaurant, casting a pondering look across at Nic picking up the menu, it was *because* they were so new to each other that they could speak like this? Or was it because they seemed to resonate with each other, despite their very different backgrounds?

Maybe we share the same resonant frequency, she thought with flickering amusement. Was that it?

She let the thought slip away, focussing only on the immediate present. On the present that was beckoning her. And on what, she was now thrillingly aware, was yet to come.

She felt her heart rate give that now familiar

little skip, a flush of warmth going through her. Life seemed good—an adventure, and different, headily so, but very good.

Thanks to her being here with Nic.

CHAPTER THREE

'OK, Doc Fran, tell me about the stars.'

Nic's invitation was just that—inviting, and Fran could not resist it. They had come out into the night, after a leisurely, easy-going Tex-Mex dinner, and taken a paved path that led up to the top of the bluff, where the lights from the resort did not reach. The low level lighting for the path showed where several benches were, and they had settled down on one. Nic's arm was around her shoulders and it felt warm, the right place for it to be.

He was lifting his face up to the heavens and so was she, and her breath caught. The night sky was ablaze, the moon not yet risen, and the stars were putting on a show that was unmatched in this clear, unpolluted air.

An exuberance filled her, fuelled by the night and the stars and the desert and their distance from her everyday life. The world she'd been born to—of castles and *palazzos* and titles and

estates—and the world she now lived in—
of arcane academia and erudite research—
seemed very far away.

And it wasn't the daiquiri running in her
veins that was making her feel elated. It had
everything to do with the warm, heavy arm
around her shoulders, the solid mass of Nic
at her side as she leant against him and gazed
upwards into the blazing glory of the heavens.

'Where do I begin?' she breathed, wondering
how to convey to Nic all that she knew, knowing it was impossible.

She knew she must start with opening his
eyes to the searing power of the universe itself.

'So—stars.' She took another breath, her
eyes lighting with her eagerness to share with
him what she knew, what she felt, what filled
her life. She waved a hand upwards. 'Fiery,
burning balls of gas, each one a powerhouse
of energy, nuclear fusion, born in stellar nurs-
eries deep in the galaxy, blazing their time,
then burning away. Some stars are small, some
huge, and how big they are, and how hot, tells
us their fate. Some—the largest—will explode
in fantastic supernovae that collapse into black

holes, while smaller ones become red giants, as our sun will one day—'

She was away, and he let her talk. She regaled him with Main Sequence and Hertzsprung-Russell and Chandrasekhar Limits and every variety of dwarf star, and neutron star and pulsars and quasars, star clusters and nebulae, until his head was spinning. And in the end he heard not her words but the passion in her voice for the subject she loved. It warmed him to do so, for passion was passion, and it could be expressed in more than cerebral enthusiasm…

His could—oh, his could, indeed!

He felt the slender weight of her body against him as they gazed upwards, so soft. The scent of her freshly washed hair caught at him, the silken fall of its lush tresses beneath his bare forearm inflaming all his senses.

Desire was kindled in him, and all of a sudden he wanted no more of stars. His free hand came to her face and he laid one finger across her lips, silencing her.

She paused, her eyes lowering to his, meeting his. Seeing in his, under the starlight, a blaze that was nothing to do with the heavens above. A blaze that lit up in her own eyes.

Her breath caught in her throat. Her gaze worked over his face. 'Enough with the stars?' she asked, and her voice was husky suddenly.

Long lashes dipped over blue eyes turned inky in the dim light. 'For now,' he answered, and the huskiness was in his voice too. His strong fingers cupped her cheek as if it were the rarest porcelain, his gaze pouring into hers. 'You love your subject so much…'

'I adore it,' she whispered.

But her hand was lifting to his face now, exploring its rough contours with the delicate tips of her fingers, tracing the planes and edges, the outline of his mouth.

'The stars will burn for aeons, for a time we cannot grasp or fathom…' her voice was still husky, a whisper, and her eyes were clinging to his, his to hers '…but this night, now, is ours.'

Slowly, sensuously, she reached her mouth to his, feeling its familiarity, its acceptance as he let her explore, slowly and sensuously, taking her time, all the time she needed, as her fingertips slid into his sable hair, cupping the nape of his sinewy neck, as his muscles flexed minutely—as, slowly and sensuously, he began to kiss her back.

How long they kissed she did not know—only knew that at some point she was drawn against his body, that strong, powerful body, folded to him as if she were silver tissue paper.

She could feel her breasts crushed, then engorged, peaking, and she gloried in it, gloried in the way his hand around her shoulder was pulling her to him, the way his mouth was foraging deep within hers, and she gloried in her answering response, eager, quickening the desire that was filling her, overwhelming her.

She heard her own voice, low in her throat, heard a kind of primitive growl in his, and then with a sudden movement he had swept her to her feet, then into his arms, as if she were a feather.

She gave a cry of laughter, exhilarated, enchanted. 'You can't carry me all the way back to the motel!'

He only laughed, carrying her down the path to the motel while she clung to him, setting her down outside the door. His hand clasping hers, he led her inside, down the corridor to his room, opening the door with a rapid swipe of the key card.

Then his arms were around her again, and he was yielding to all the overpowering impulses of his heated desire for her, setting it ablaze in her as a heady exhilaration filled her. Whatever it was that was happening between them, she was giving herself to it totally, consumingly.

A bedside lamp was all that illuminated the room, softening its contours as he drew her towards the waiting bed. A sense of rightness filled him that they were coming together now, like this. Whatever it was about this beautiful, breathtaking woman, she was right for him.

And *this* was right, what he was doing, sliding his hands on either side of her face, feeling the softness of her hair, her skin, gazing down at her with desire in his eyes, and warmth, and something more than both.

For one long moment he just gazed at her, into those clear grey eyes which showed she had made the decision to be here with him, now.

For this.

For his mouth slowly moving down to hers,

kissing her slowly, carefully, to start the union that they would make together.

She answered his kiss, gave herself to it, and he folded her to him. Her arms moved around the strong column of his body. She felt him surge against her, and whilst a little ripple of shock went through her in its wake came a shiver of excitement. His desire for her was blatant, and she welcomed it. She felt her breasts cresting against his hard-muscled chest and knew he felt her reaction to him. Heard the low laugh of pleasure in her pleasure.

Slowly, sensuously, he peeled her clothes from her, never taking his eyes from hers, letting her delicate hands perform the same intimate office for him.

He let her do what she realised she had been aching to do—run the palms of her hands over his bare, smooth, taut-muscled torso, glorying in its muscled strength. And for answer he cupped the small weight of her swelling breasts with his hands, thumbs lifting to their cresting peaks.

She gave a moan in her throat, dropping back her head at the arousal of the sensation. Desire quickened in her, a sense of urgency, and in that same harmony that united them he was pressing her back down upon the coverlet of the bed, drawing it back so they lay upon the sheets.

Italian words broke from him as he gazed down at her perfect body, expressing his desire for her, telling her how beautiful she was, and she answered with a sensuous smile, for of course she understood his husky praise, answered it with her own for him. She lifted her hands to run them once more over that glorious torso, to glide them downwards over his taut, muscled abs and then, with a little gasp, realised just how very, very ready for her he was.

He laughed, collapsing down beside her, rolling her on to him so that she gasped again, then quickened, heat surging in her. His hand was around her nape, drawing her eager mouth to his, feasting on its sweet delights. She moved upon him, and with another groan he flipped her back on to the sheets, coming over her. His hands clasped hers, high on the pillow, and her hair was like a flag, blazoning her welcome of what was to come.

His eyes poured into hers. 'Fran…' He said her name, nothing more. And in it was a question—he wanted her to be sure, so very sure, that this was what she wanted.

She could sense his absolute self-control, his absolute assurance that nothing would happen that she did not want, did not want to share, totally and consumingly, with him.

She lifted her mouth to his. Kissed him softly, sensuously. Then she let her head fall back upon the pillow. Still gazing up at him. Knowing what she wanted. Knowing absolutely.

It was all the answer he needed.

Slowly, with infinite precision, he lowered himself to her, and with a response as old as time her thighs slackened, letting him find what he so urgently sought. She opened to him, feeling her body flower, all her blood surge in a swelling tide. Her heated flesh fitted around his strength, enclosing him within her, feeling the power of him, the desire of him for her, for her body, for her answering desire of him.

She felt her spine lift, arching towards his body as it reared over hers. Her crested nipples grazed his torso so that he gave a groan, his fingers meshing with hers yet more tightly. The strong cords of his neck, the tensed line of his jaw—all told her how very, very near release he was.

Yet he waited for her. Waited for her to make slow, exploratory movements of her hips, to feel him full and engorged within her, to feel the rightness of him being so, the sensual pleasure of it. With every slow, deliberate movement she made she could feel the tide of her desire mounting within her, heat rising within her, dissolving her into him until, in a vast upwelling of unstoppable sensation, they ran together, flooding out into the wholeness of her body, sweeping through her, consuming her, possessing her...

She heard her voice cry out, felt her neck arching, and heard his own roar of release, felt the spasming of his hands on hers, the surging pulse of his body within hers, carrying them forward, onward, into the vast unknown, into what bound them, body to body, to blaze and burn together.

Time stopped. Everything stopped. There was only this now, this possession, this fusion, this glory of desire fulfilled, passion sated upon passion, binding them together, making them one...

Until slowly, infinitely slowly, time began again, and now she could feel the pounding of her heart, of his, as their bodies slackened. And now he was cradling her trembling body, moving away from her only to draw her back against him, his strong hands tender on her, his breath warm on her shoulder as he held her until her body lay still and quiet with his.

Softly he eased the tangled tendrils of her hair back from her face, kissing her cheekbone gently, murmuring low words she could not hear for the ebbing drumming in her ears, the heartbeat that was quietening finally.

Peace, a wondrous peace, filled her. The peace of fulfilment, of a contentment that seemed to be in every atom of her being, body and mind and soul. She could feel his powerful body, relaxed, exhausted in the aftermath of the overpowering intensity of their union.

A slow, tender smile eased her lips and then her eyelids were fluttering closed and sleep, so necessary, was sweeping up over her like the softest cashmere, embracing her as sweetly as did his slackening arms around her.

In the cradle of the night they slept...in the cradle of their embrace of each other.

* * *

'OK,' said Nic, 'all set for the Grand Canyon?'

They were having brunch at the buffet bar of the motel—late, for theirs had been a long, *long* lie-in. Fran's thoughts skittered away from just what that lie-in had entailed, lest it make her want to rebook the room.

A kind of wonder filled her—wonder that the night that had passed had been like *nothing* she had ever experienced. Her eyes fastened on the man sitting opposite her, his lithe, power-ful frame relaxed, indolent, even. But then *he* was like no other man ever could be.

He was relaxing back with an air of well-being about him, and she knew perfectly well what the cause of that was. Because she shared it with him—as they had shared their passion, their fulfilment, and now would share the day that was to come.

And what would come after? Her mind sheered away from that question. There was no point thinking about what might happen 'after'—they would take it a day at a time, a night at a time. That was all she wanted right now. And it was more than enough.

She felt delight flood through her—a sense

of carefree happiness that came from what she was doing, indulging in this adventure with a man whose lazy glance could make her heart beat faster even before he reached for her.

She felt again that lift that came whenever she looked at him, thought about him, felt a smile play on her lips, her gaze soften. Her pulse quickened. She didn't know, could not tell just why it was like this with him, knew only that it was what she wanted.

Nic had swept her away, and here she was, at his side, on the road trip of a lifetime—an adventure she would embrace with all her will. She hadn't sought it, but it was here and now—with Nic.

That lift came again, the rush of happiness.

'North Rim or South?' Nic was saying now. 'South means we could take in Vegas if you wanted?'

Fran shook her head vigorously in rejection. Nic was glad. He'd prefer to avoid Vegas himself. Though he had no property there, there was always a chance he might be recognised if they stayed at one of the major hotels.

A thought struck him—one that intruded into his good mood.

'Is it somewhere your ex-fiancé would have taken you?' he heard himself ask.

Hell, why had he said that? It made him sound possessive—and he was never possessive about women. Nor did he let them get possessive about *him*, either.

There was no point. No point in a woman wanting commitment from him.

No point in a woman wanting commitment from any man.

Hadn't his poor mother hammered that home to him, her own sorry life story grim proof of that? Men let women down…they didn't stick around. They cut and ran when it suited them, when the woman tried to get possessive, wanted commitment from them.

With a jolt out of his dark reverie he realised that Fran had given a choked laugh in response. *'Cesare?'* she said, again giving his name the Italian pronunciation. 'Las Vegas would have been the *last* place he'd have visited!'

Cesare would loathe Las Vegas—*far* too vulgar and touristy for his aristocratic tastes.

'Is he an astrophysicist too?' Nic heard himself ask. He wondered why he was going on about the man.

'Oh, heavens no! Cesare is...' Fran paused, trying to find a way to describe him to Nic. 'Well, I guess you could say he works on the land.'

That was true enough. Cesare ran his vast estates with businesslike efficiency, as well as a proprietorial stewardship that took responsibility for his ancient heritage.

Nic gave a satisfied laugh. 'A hick? A—what's that particular English term? Oh, yes—a country bumpkin!' It was good to think of the unknown Cesare as some kind of plodding farm boy.

'Mmm...' murmured Fran equivocally.

She really needed to change the subject. La Donna Francesca, once engaged to Cesare, Il Conte di Mantegna, had no place here in this egalitarian country. Here, she was only Doc Fran Ristori.

And Nic was Nic Rossi, who ran the security team at the Falcone Nevada.

And that's what I want—here and now. Nothing else. Just him and me—for while it lasts.

'OK, we'll skip Vegas,' Nic said now, his laid-back, laconic style already so endearingly familiar to her.

He drank some coffee and made a face. Fran smiled sympathetically. 'Your Italian genes are showing again,' she said, amused. 'I've lived Stateside a few years now, and still the coffee is grim!'

He laughed, lines indenting around his mouth. This was tricky territory—she was taking him for Italian-American, and he wanted to keep it that way. Wanted to stay as simple Nic Rossi, who had worked his way up from a deadbeat childhood to a respectable career in hotel security.

He stretched out his legs and returned to the subject of the Grand Canyon. 'How about West Rim?' he suggested. 'The Hualapai Reservation does helicopter flights, a skywalk and a river ride. Plus we can stay in one of the cabins there tonight if we want.'

Fran's face lit. 'Sounds wonderful!' Then she paused. 'But pricey... I'll go halves with you.'

Nic was touched. Just as he had been when she'd asked him, before they'd set out for the Array, to charge the SUV hire against her room. He'd waved it away, said he'd fix it, and left it at that. She hadn't pressed and he was glad.

'Deal,' he answered, and they busied themselves making their reservations before getting on the road.

It was an unforgettable experience when they got there, reducing them both to awed silence. They stood at the canyon's edge, in the heat and the silence, looking across to the far North Rim, seemingly so close, but actually ten miles away across the great chasm in the earth, the dramatic formations of rocks and cliffs, the narrow ribbon of river far, far below, the great arching sky above.

They did not speak, only found each other's hands and stood, fingers meshed, together, side by side. Then another group of tourists came up behind them and Fran stepped aside, slipped her hand from Nic's to let them by.

Nic found himself glancing down at his hand. It felt empty without Fran's in it.

He shook his head to clear it. It was the effect of this place, that was all.

They headed back to eat lunch under an airy

awning before their flight down into the canyon, then a boat trip, gliding sedately along the Colorado river, deceptively calm in this stretch, gazing up at the towering cliffs above slowly passing them by.

'Fancy white water rafting next?' Nic asked wickedly.

'No, thank you!' Fran said primly. 'This is quite fast enough for me.'

He laughed, relaxing with her. Resting his arm around her shoulder in a gesture that seemed to come naturally to them as she leaned into him companionably.

Back up on the rim again, they made their way to their SUV, which was looking decidedly dusty by now. It had come a long way.

And so have I, she thought.

Her mind skittered away, not wanting to ponder or analyse. She just wanted to enjoy this adventure and wherever it took her.

'OK,' she said as they strapped themselves in, turning on the air-con with relief, 'where to now?'

'Shall we aim for the North Rim?' Nic said. 'It's a long drive, but we could give it a go.'

'Let's do it!' she said, settling back happily.

The sense of exhilaration that she was getting used to filled her again. Crazy this might be, but she wanted it! She was not thinking beyond it—just going along for the ride. With Nic at her side.

In the end they didn't head straight for the North Rim. Instead they diverted to meander into the vast Canyonlands of Utah, making their way along the well-trodden tourist trail, taking in the Grand Staircase, Zion and Bryce, stopping over at lodges, hotels and motels along the way.

They were taking it easy, each day a new adventure, for now putting aside their own lives, their existence beyond this road trip romance.

They did some short, easy-access hiking trails, nothing strenuous, buying the kit they needed as they went, and they did a lot of driving through the awe-inspiring, breathtaking scenery all around, stopping as and when they felt like it. Unpressured, leisurely…

Days slipped by, each one bringing its own delights. And each night was as burningly passionate as the first had been. As if by silent mutual consent neither of them counted the days, wanting nothing more than to reach the next awe-inspiring destination. Never looking further ahead than the next day. Never thinking about what would happen when, finally, they ran out of road. Ran out of time.

It was at a small, cabin-style café, where they'd stopped for leisurely coffee and donuts one mid-morning, as they were finally heading back south towards the North Rim, where both the road and their time together finally ended.

Fran had been deliberately keeping her phone off except to look ahead to their next impromptu destination, which she was doing now, to see what accommodation they might book before finishing their drive to the National Park north of the Grand Canyon the next day.

Usually there were no messages, but today, as she switched on the phone, a flurry of texts, missed calls and voicemails greeted her. She would have ignored them but she could see the identity of the sender. It was her brother, Tonio.

She frowned, starting to read his texts with growing anxiety. Not noticing that Nic, like her, was checking his phone as well, and his expression was changing too.

The message on his screen demanded his attention. But it was bad timing. Bad timing to get a heads-up from his business development manager that a potential prime site was likely to become available in Manhattan. He would need to check it out personally and move fast. Immediately.

But protest reared in him. He didn't want to call time on being with Fran.

I don't want this to end! Not yet.

Even as the protest sounded in his head he felt hard, cold rational thought pour down on it.

So how long do you want it to last? How long before it ends? Just how much more do you want of this—of her, of Fran? Another week? Two weeks? How long? How long to put your life on hold while you drive around the American West?

His eyes bored into the screen, willing the message to disappear. But it was still there. His real life was summoning him back. This hedonistic R&R, unscheduled, snatched out of his life, this instinctive, overriding diversion with this incredible woman who had blazed across his path was over.

Dimly, he realised that Fran was speaking, and he switched his attention to her. Her voice was hollow, her eyes filled with fearful emotion. For a second, just a split second, he thought it must be because he'd said out loud that their time was over.

But it was not that.

'Nic...' The strain was naked in her words. 'Nic, my grandfather...he's had a heart attack. They—they don't think he's going to pull through.' Her voice wobbled at the end, choking.

Instantly, instinctively, he reached across the table to take her hand. She looked at him, her fingers clutching at his.

'I have to go to England,' she said. 'My mother is there already, and my brother and sister. My father is on his way too. I—I have to be there.'

He nodded. The decision was made. The only decision to make. He beckoned to the server, wanting to pay and go.

In minutes they were back in the SUV, heading south.

'We can make McCarran in Vegas in just over three hours, I think. Can you sort a plane ticket while we drive?'

Fran nodded numbly. It was unreal, surely, what was happening? Her grandfather, who had seemed to be as indestructible as the ancient ducal castle that was his principal seat, was dying. By the time she got there it might be too late.

Guilt smote her. She'd kept her distance from her family ever since breaking up with Cesare, not wanting to hear any more of her mother's recriminations for doing so, burying herself in her work, devoting herself to her research.

Her guilt was exacerbated by realising that the last thing she wanted her mother to know was that she had taken off on a crazy road trip with a guy who worked in security at a hotel.

She felt emotion twist inside her. This adventure with Nic had been a mad, impetuous break out of time—away from all that she knew. It had been heady, and fantastic, and wonderful.

But it had nothing to do with her real life, did it? Neither the sober life she lived as a scientist in the halls of academe, nor the life she had been born to as Donna Francesca.

The life she was being summoned back to now, to what might be the deathbed of her grandfather, the centre of her mother's family, who even now might be passing his ducal coronet to his successor—her uncle—while his son-in-law—her father the Marchese—would be paying the respects due from one nobleman to another.

And she must be there too—she *must*. Whatever the friction with her mother, it counted for nothing at a time like this.

Blindly, she stared out of the tinted windows of the SUV at the wild, rugged landscape they were passing through. It had become so familiar in the past amazing, unforgettable days she had spent there, spent with the man who was now at the wheel, driving her to Las Vegas airport with all the speed the law allowed.

I don't want to leave this—to lose this.

It was a cry that came from within, from a place she hadn't known existed until that moment. But it was a cry she must silence.

And if not now, then when?

That was the knowledge that pressed upon her. Had her brother's messages not summoned her away, what would it have gained her? Another few days with Nic? Maybe another week at most? How could it have lasted longer than that? Her other real life would have called her back. She had things to do. Papers to write. Another research post to find, maybe a move to another city—another country, even.

So maybe this sudden ending of her time with Nic was for the best. Wasn't it? Yet something seemed to twist inside her, like a heavy stone turning over...

Nic was talking and she made herself listen. He was telling her not to worry about her suitcase, left at the Falcone Nevada, that he would ensure it reached her office.

She thanked him absently, her hands clenched in her lap. She urged the SUV onwards, towards the airport, anxiety filling her lest she arrive in London too late. But even as she urged it onward she knew that the last of her time with Nic was ticking away.

Their parting, when they arrived at McCarran, was swift. She was cutting it fine for the flight she'd booked, and there was no time for anything more than for her to take Nic's hands as he helped her to the concourse at Departures and press them tightly.

'Thank you!'

Her words were vehement, her kiss swift, pressing his mouth so fleetingly he had no time to do what he wanted, to yank her into his arms and crush her to him one last time.

But the last time had been and gone, without either of them knowing it. So she slipped her hands from his, slung on the backpack she'd acquired on their road trip, gripped her passport. She had already checked in online, had no luggage to drop, and she needed to make her flight now—right *now.*

Unable to bear to look back at him, she forged forward through the opening doors, was swallowed up inside.

For one endless moment he stared after her, not believing she was gone.

Then, making his muscles work, feeling a sudden clenching in his stomach, he swung away, back to the SUV, gunned the engine. He drove off. Heading back to the Falcone Nevada.

It was over. His time with Fran was done. His expression tightened, and he wondered why he felt as if he'd just been punched in the guts...

CHAPTER FOUR

BY THE TIME she arrived at Beaucourt Castle, her grandfather's principal seat, it was late morning.

Her young sister Adrietta ran up to Fran as she climbed wearily out of the Rolls-Royce sent to collect her from Heathrow, hugging her and exclaiming, 'He's rallying! He told the doctor to take himself off and he wanted lobster for lunch! Washed down with claret!'

Fran gave a tired, relieved smile. 'He's a tough old boot,' she said fondly.

They made their way to her grandfather's bedroom where, somewhere in the huge, crimson tester bed, her grandfather was propped upright, looking frail, testy, but blessedly alive—even though he was wired up to all kinds of medical kit and a nurse was hovering.

'So they got you here too, did they?' the Duke barked as he saw her, but his voice was hoarse and his face had aged and, despite the defiance of his attitude, Fran knew she'd done the right thing in hastening here.

However wrenched away from Nic she felt.

No, she must not think of that. Must not think, as she had for the ten-hour duration of her flight, of Nic making his way back to the Falcone, sorting her things to be sent on to the West Coast. Must not think of him doing his job, putting on his tuxedo for the evening, resuming his duties. Must not think of him at all.

She felt a strange tearing inside her—a hollowing out. But she knew she must set it aside. Now she must focus on her family, on her indomitable grandfather who had pulled through, and who, even if lobster and claret were most certainly *not* on the menu today, nor for some weeks to come, was still very much here.

He was commanding the scene, as he always did, ordering her mother to stop fussing and fretting, telling her uncle the Marquess he must make do with his courtesy title yet awhile, that the ducal coronet was going nowhere for now.

And there was relief for Fran for another reason too. Her mother, her face tear-stained, had swept her into a clinging embrace.

'Darling, I'm so, *so* glad you came! Thank you…*thank you*!'

'Of *course* I came.' Fran had hugged her mother back.

It was all that had been said, but Fran knew that her estrangement from her mother was over. It had been helped, she soon realised, not just by her grandfather's close call with death, but also by the news that was clearly serving to divert her mother from endlessly bewailing Fran's decision not to marry Cesare.

Adrietta was getting engaged to a highly suitable *parti*, heir to a *visconti*—which gave the Marchesa the enjoyable prospect of organising a lavish engagement party and an even more lavish wedding the following year.

Fran was relieved, glad both for her mother and her sister. But her mood was strange. She was being absorbed back into her family, into the world, she'd been born into. Yet it jarred—the contrast between her days now at Beaucourt and how her days so short a time ago with Nic, cruising the American West, could not have been greater.

She told none of her family about him. Tried not to think about him. They had had a road trip romance—brief, impulsive and carefree. It had never been intended to be anything more. Their time together must become a precious memory.

Yet, in the long reaches of the night she could feel her body ache for his as she lay in her bed in the room that was always hers whenever she visited Beaucourt Castle.

As the days passed, and her grandfather gradually regained his strength, her time with Nic receded more and more. She was absorbed into her existence as Donna Francesca, with her parents, her siblings, her aunt, uncle and her cousins, all accepting her presence again easily—just one more member of the close-knit family spread between England and Italy.

With her grandfather robustly on the mend, her parents and siblings decided to head back to Italy. Fran went with them, to spend a week at the eighteenth-century *palazzo* in Lombardy that was her childhood home, before returning to her university, now that both her vacation and her compassionate leave were over.

She told her parents she would be looking for another research post, and this drew from her mother the hope that she would find one in Europe this time. And, even better, find a replacement for the fiancé she had discarded so cavalierly.

'I just want you to be *happy*, darling!' her mother exclaimed.

'I *am* happy. I'm happy in my work,' Fran replied.

'Oh, it's not the *same*,' her mother protested. 'Look how happy Adrietta is! She's radiant! I want that for you, too, my darling girl. I want there to be that special man in your life who is like no other that you have known!'

Fran did not answer. Thoughts flickered in her head, memories flashing…

Her mother pounced. 'You're thinking of Cesare, aren't you?'

'No!' Fran's refutation was instant. Instinctive. It had not been Cesare in her head. In her memory. It had been a quite different man.

No. The admonition to herself came swiftly. She had taken off with Nic because it had confirmed that Cesare was in the past and she was free to indulge herself. But the point about indulgence, she had to remind herself sternly, was that that was *all* it was. The easy companionship and casual camaraderie that had been between her and Nic from the off, and all that hot desire for his strong, tough body that had melted her in his searing embrace, had passed.

It's been and gone. It was good, but it's over.

It made sense to tell herself that, to remind herself of that when she was back in her department, working on her next paper, teaching her assigned batch of undergrads, looking out for new research posts. Made sense to tell herself that just as she had accepted that Cesare was no longer in her life, so she would accept the same of Nic—she had let Cesare go easily enough, so it would be the same with Nic.

Yes, it made sense. But it had caused a pang, all the same, to find her suitcase from the Falcone Nevada beside her desk, delivered as promised by Nic. Suddenly vivid in her head was that last farewell to him, in the hectic anxiety of her departure from the airport at Las Vegas. Even more vivid was the sensation of that last farewell kiss, so hurried and fleeting.

But maybe it was good that it had ended so abruptly. Road trips could not go on for ever. In time, the vivid memories would fade. She would move on with her life. She must.

Yet as she called up on her screen a complex

set of graphs depicting the interactions of the data she was examining her mind went momentarily blank.

A stray, random thought drifted across it. *We never did get to North Rim, did we?*

Their road trip had stopped before that. And for a moment, before she bent her mind to focus on the graphs again, that seemed a cause for regret.

As if something remained unfinished...

Nic picked up the thirty-thousand-euro gold pen that lay on his fifty-thousand-euro eighteenth-century desk in his office and scrawled his strong, incisive signature—*Falcone*—onto the purchase contract in front of him.

The prime Manhattan site was his. It had cost him top dollar, as would the refurb and the launch, but he didn't care. It would be worth it. For a few brief months last year he'd enjoyed rebranding the Viscari Manhattan, but that had been ripped from him. Now he had a flagship property of his own, and no one could take it from him.

Setting down the pen, he waited for a sense

of satisfaction at such a signal acquisition to fill him.

Instead, memory flickered in his head, of how he'd signed that bar chit in the Falcone Nevada in the summer, keeping his name from the sight of the woman beside him.

Instantly the view before him, overlooking the ancient city of Rome which had spawned him in its slums and now housed him in a High Renaissance former papal *palazzo*, the headquarters of Falcone, vanished. In its place, as vivid as if he were there, was a wild landscape, rocky and bare, sun-scorched, parched and desolate, or darkly forested land, pine trees towering all around him, and he and Fran driving through it, day after day, the road ahead always stretching endlessly, taking them wherever they wanted, over the next horizon, and the next—as if their journey together would never end.

Except that it had—the road had forked, and they had gone their separate ways. She to study the arcane mysteries of the universe, he to soar ever higher with Falcone.

More memory pierced—of that feeling of having been punched in the guts, winded, as he'd watched Fran hurry through into Departures at McCarran. He felt it again now, and in his head he heard his own thoughts coming in its wake.

Should I get in touch? Arrange to see her again?

Because they had been good together.

The anodyne description flared like a struck match in his body's memory, flaming into heat, instantly recalling all their days and their nights, making him shift restlessly. It would be easy to make contact again, to track her down at her university. All he had to do was pick up the phone.

But his hand stayed where it was. He made it stay.

Let it go—let her *go. There is no purpose in making contact. What there was, was good— but it has gone. Its course has run. Move on.*

He always moved on. All his affairs were transient. He would not risk anything else. In his head he heard his mother, scarred by what life had done to her, lamenting the infidelity of men. Of the man who had seduced her then left her pregnant and alone, a prey to other men.

'You'll be the same,' she would say to him

sorrowfully. *'You look so like him...so hand-some! But so faithless—'*

His mouth thinned. Well, he would *not* be like his unknown father—because he would never let a woman expect anything of him.

And Fran—would she have expected any-thing more of me, more than what we had?

He did not know, but it was best not to ask the question. Best not to ask how she would be once she knew he was not Nic Rossi, who worked in security at the Falcone Nevada, but Nicolo Falcone. It would inevitably come out if he contacted her again. It would mean ex-planations, complications...

No, best to let their brief time together fade into the past, where it belonged. The best place for it to be. The best place for *her* to be.

Fran gazed at the packed-up boxes of her pos-sessions in her West Coast rental apartment, ready for freighting back to the UK, her emo-tions mixed. She had finally taken another re-search post—a temporary position at her old Cambridge college, which had delighted her mother. Fran's own feelings were less cer-tain—ultra-prestigious though Cambridge would always be, it seemed to be a step back into her past, into the life, the world, she'd come from.

In America she felt freer—free to be only Dr Fran Ristori, not La Donna Francesca as well... Free to take off on an impulsive road trip with a guy she'd met at a hotel—one of the staff there.

In her head sounded the affectionate nickname Nic had bestowed upon her—Doc Fran. Yes, with him she had been that, too, and it had endeared him to her. She felt her lips twitch in a fond smile at the memory.

Emotion swirled again inside her, disquieting. Leaving America would set the final seal on that impetuous romance. Was that truly what she wanted? In the months that had passed since her time with Nic she knew that for all her admonitions to herself she'd never quite been able to let go entirely of wondering about him—wondering whether she should, after all, attempt to get in touch.

The question had hovered at the edges of her mind, however many times she'd told herself it was best to accept it had been a fling, nothing more than that. Wonderful, memorable, joyous—but only for the duration of their road trip. It couldn't be anything more.

Yet the question came again, and her hand, she realised, was hovering over her phone.

Maybe I just want to say goodbye. To let him know I'm leaving the States. To reach closure. Closure? Or...?

Was that the reason? She didn't know. Didn't want to hear the voice inside her head telling her that if Nic had wanted to get in touch with her, if *he* had not wanted to accept it was over, then he'd had plenty of opportunity to do so. He could have found her through her university, easily.

But he hasn't, has he? He's moved on— clearly and obviously moved on.

But something plucked at her all the same... that flickering emotion she knew she should quell.

As if of its own accord, her hand picked up her phone. She found the hotel's number, dialled it...

Two minutes later she was disconnecting again, emotions twisting inside her. The receptionist, polite as she had been, had been adamant that there was no Nic Rossi working at the Nevada hotel, nor at any Falcone hotel.

Fran stared blankly into space. A hollow feeling was forming inside her. Nic had left the Falcone with no trace.

He could be anywhere.

And 'anywhere' was the same as 'nowhere'. She felt the hollow inside her increasing. In practical terms she had no idea where he was, or how to find him.

She stared at her empty living room, filled only with sealed boxes. Just as sealed as, she realised, the time she had spent all those weeks ago with Nic.

Sealed into the past.

Where it would have to stay.

Nic was in London, at his residence in the Falcone Mayfair.

The hotel was an elegant, double-fronted Georgian town mansion, occupying the south side of a fashionable square, and its possession had meant he had been content to leave the rival Viscari property in nearby St James's in the Viscari portfolio during the brief period of daggers-drawn co-ownership last year.

As it happened, though, he would be visiting the Viscari St James's this very evening, attending as the plus-one of the up-and-coming designer responsible for the Viscari's lavish new roof garden, the launch of which was the occasion for a glitzy party.

Nic, obviously, given the acrimony between himself and Vito Viscari over Falcone's short-lived corporate raid last year, was not on the extensive and exclusive guest list, but that did not trouble him. He merely wanted to evaluate Lorna Linhurst's horticultural design skills with a possible view to using them on his own hotels—as he had already intimated to her.

What he had *not* yet intimated to her was the fact that he was considering taking a more than professional interest in her.

He shifted restlessly, tugging on the cuffs of his tuxedo, his mood just as restless. Maybe it was time he had another affair. The months since his road trip with Fran had been intense and full on, his priority focussed on opening the brand new Falcone Manhattan. It had absorbed him completely, along with his already ongoing programme of acquisitions, and R&R

had taken a back seat. But now, surely, it was time to finally move on from Fran.

Lorna Linhurst could be just the woman to move on with. Divorced, in her late twenties, highly attractive, a good figure—what was not to like? Not to desire?

He told himself that again as they made their way into the Viscari St James's a short while later. Lorna was appealingly dressed in a dark red evening gown, her chestnut hair carefully styled. She seemed a little tense this evening, but that was to be expected. She was showing off her abilities to a potentially highly valuable client.

Yes, there was nothing to object to in her— she was intelligent and very attractive. Except she wasn't Fran.

Nic was well aware that his presence as Lorna's plus one had not gone unnoticed, and it gave him a stab of satisfaction.

But he blandly ignored the staff member who had admitted them to the elevator that was to sweep them up to the roof garden as he promptly got on his mobile phone—presumably to alert his boss that Nicolo Falcone had just strolled in. He wasn't here to see that pampered playboy Vito Viscari holding court, he was here to see what his rival had achieved, and whether to poach his garden designer from him if he sufficiently liked what she'd done.

As they emerged on to the roof garden Nic could see in an instant that it was a triumph of design—a green haven high above the London traffic on this mild autumnal evening. He let Lorna take him around, let her explain how she'd coped with the inherent difficulties of creating a garden on a functioning roof, making trickling rivulets out of drainage channels and disguising ventilation shafts with skilful plantings.

They reached the far side of the garden and Nic paused, glancing down at her. 'Draw up some initial ideas for refreshing the gardens at the Falcone Firenze,' he said. He made his voice warm, less businesslike. 'We'll discuss them over lunch sometime.'

He saw her face light with pleasure at the potential commission—and at such a prestigious property. It confirmed his decision. Florence would be an ideal location to pursue an R&R interest in her as well as a professional one. It might be just what he needed to cure his restlessness.

His eyes rested on her a moment. On the rich chestnut hair, deep-set eyes, generous mouth. She would be very easy to take to bed. But was that what he really wanted?

Being with Lorna would do the job of finally moving him on. Put that brief fleeting time with Fran out of his head and close the door on it firmly, decisively. Fran had been different—his time with her had been different—but that changed nothing. He didn't *do* relationships. He did R&R, and kept it to that. Fran, however memorable, had been just one more round.

And now, surely, it was time to start another. Potentially with the woman at his side this evening.

Nic's gaze lifted from Lorna, moved out across the expanse of the rooftop garden to the throng of guests, most of whom were gathered on the wide white-paved area in front of the long conservatory that housed the rooftop restaurant, softly lit, with concealed lighting creating a stage effect from where he stood on the less lit edge of the garden.

His eyes panned across the chattering guests,

over the waiters circulating with silver trays of champagne flutes and canapés. He could see Vito Viscari, busy circulating, meeting and greeting his guests, distinctive with his slim elegance and height, letting the female guests bestow effusive air kisses on him, effortlessly charming them with his matinee idol looks.

An expression of casual contempt for how easy the cossetted handsome heir to the Viscari dynasty had had it all his gilded life crossed Nic's hardening face.

He shifted position restlessly. He had seen what he'd come to see and now he'd take his leave. Lorna, doubtless, would want to stay on, enjoy her creative triumph.

Then, just as he was about to tell her he was leaving, the shifting pattern of the throng changed. Nic's gaze froze.

Out of the mass of guests one distilled into focus.

A tall, slender woman in a long deep blue gown, her hair in elaborate coils on her head, an embroidered silk shawl over her elbows, was talking to two other people. A woman he had last seen disappearing into the Departures hall of McCarran airport in Las Vegas. A woman he had not thought to ever see again.

And immediately, piercingly, two thoughts plunged into his brain.

He had not moved on at all.

And Lorna Linhurst had ceased to exist for him.

Fran smiled, listening to Cesare's wife Carla telling her something amusing about her infant son. Beside them, Cesare was looking down at his wife, with an expression in his eyes that had never come Fran's way in all the time she'd known him—not even in their brief engagement.

She shifted position, feeling restless suddenly, confined by the close-fitting haute couture evening gown from one of her favourite Milan designers. Her sapphire necklace—also a favourite, bestowed upon her by her father for her twenty-first birthday from the di Ristori vaults—was heavy around her throat. She was in full make-up, her hair professionally styled in an ornate fashion. It felt strange to be so dressed up once more, disporting herself at opulent affairs like this party tonight.

Even though she was now back at Cambridge, she was keeping her social life to a minimum. She went to visit her grandfather from time to time at Beaucourt, glad that he was steadily getting back to his old, irascible self, and before Christmas she would be flying out to Italy for her sister's engagement party—a huge bash that her mother and Adrietta were revelling in.

But she'd come back to England to go to Cambridge and work, not to party. Tonight was an exception.

She was here with Cesare and Carla at this lavish do at the Viscari St James's because it was owned by Carla's step-cousin, Vito. Fran's own cousin, Harry, the young Earl of Cranleigh, was here as well, as her partner, and all of them were adding an aristocratic cachet to the glittering, high-society evening at Carla's request.

Now Carla was thanking her for coming.

'I always do what I can to support Vito,' Carla said frankly to her.

'Well, that's what families are for.' Fran smiled. 'And friends,' she added, throwing an affectionate glance towards Cesare.

She would always count him as a friend, and

only felt relief to discover how much in love he was with Carla, so that she knew breaking her engagement to him had been a welcome release.

That sense of restlessness came again. She had given up Cesare easily, eager to plunge into the excitement of working with a Nobel Laureate. Thinking no more of him. A frown creased her brows. She had thought more about Nic than she ever had about Cesare.

Nic, with his searing blue eyes that crinkled when he smiled his wolf smile at her, laughed with her, and swept her into his strong arms to kiss her until she was breathless with desire for him.

She tore her mind away. Since accepting that he was gone from her life, that he belonged only in the past and that her life had moved on, she had tried not to think of him, not to remember their time together. She had sought to ignore the flickering emotions that came from time to time, uninvited—little eddies that swirled like dust devils, stirring up her memories.

Cesare was asking about her new research post, and Carla was mentioning something about the Fitzwilliam Museum in Cambridge and its artworks of the High Renaissance—the subject she wrote about in her professional life.

Fran listened with only half an ear, distracted by the dust devils of memory she had just stirred up, seeking to still them. She swept her eyes out and around, determined to divert her thoughts away from pointless memories of Nic. She was here, in London, and Nic was thousands of miles away and in the past. Where he must stay.

Her gaze threaded through the mass of guests, past the paved terrace with its tables and benches, the stone-rimmed pools and trickling rivulets, along the little pathways lined with topiary, onward towards the fenced perimeter at the roof's edge.

And stopped dead.

Two people were standing there at the intersection of two pathways. One, a woman in a dark red evening gown, was half turned towards the man beside her—a man in a tuxedo, like all the other men present. A man who was like no other man present. A man who should not be here. Could not be here—not in London, not here, a few dozen metres away from her.

But he *was*.

And in the bare handful of seconds it took Fran to see him, for her brain to recognise him, she knew with a rush of emotion that was a sudden whirlwind inside her that should not be there, even as *he* should not be here, that something had leapt within her.

Joy.

Nic started forward—then halted. She had seen him. He'd seen it in her face, the sudden recognition in her gaze.

He felt his stomach clench, his mind blank. He wasn't prepared for this. He felt numbed, as if someone had just slugged him in the solar plexus, knocking the wind from him. For a second he could not move. Then, like an automaton, he turned to the woman at his side.

'Excuse me a moment.' His voice came from very far away.

He started forward again. Fran was walking towards him, making her way down a path bordered by a low box hedge either side, her stride quickening on her high heels. She came up to him as he stepped towards her, closing the distance between them.

'*Nic!* What on *earth* are you doing here!' The exclamation in her voice matched the astonishment in her face, in her widened eyes.

Was there more than astonishment in them? Nic thought, feeling again that slug to the solar plexus as his eyes met hers, seeing that sudden leap of expression in them. For a second, nothing else existed.

Then, like another slug, realisation hit him—that seeing her again, here, like this, was going to mean an instant revealing of himself. There was no time for anything else. No time to do anything but fasten his eyes on her, feel the rush of adrenaline in his body, catch the scent of her hair, all so familiar, crowding back into his consciousness as if it had been only yesterday that he'd parted with her. As if the months between had simply vanished.

Dimly, he realised she was speaking again.

'Are you working *here* now?' she was asking. 'At Viscari?'

Her mind was tumbling over itself, incoherence in her jangling thoughts. Was that why she hadn't been able to trace him at Falcone? Because he had swapped employers? But the reasons for his vanishing weren't what was preoccupying her—it was the soaring of her emotions like fireworks going off inside her.

Nic! Oh, Nic! His name sang in her head as her eyes fastened on him, clung almost tangibly to his form, his real, solid frame. He was here, here right in front of her! And it was *good*—oh, more than good to see him again! It was *wonderful*!

All her endless telling herself that it had been just a fleeting romance, that that was all it *should* be, that she had to let him slip away into the past, all melted like ice on a hot stove, evaporating instantly.

That was the truth filling her now, pushing out all the arguments to herself that she'd marshalled to justify why their road trip had had to end. Now, seeing him so tall, so solid, so *real*—so close…

Blood was rushing to her cheeks, leaping in her veins. She felt that same immediate, primitive response she'd given when she'd first set eyes on him, that instinctive, instant *Wow!* as she'd felt the hit of his physical impact on her. She could feel it again now, as unstoppable as the hot, surging memories that assailed her.

Nic, his mouth velvet on hers, melting her bones.

Nic, his arms strong about her, sweeping her off to bed.

Nic, his body arching over hers, caressing hers, possessing her, taking her to places that had made her cry out with ecstasy...

It was all vivid in her head, her consciousness. The searing reality of his presence in front of her was so absolutely, totally unexpected—so absolutely, totally wonderful!

It took her a moment, in the rush to her brain, the leap in her blood, to realise that he wasn't answering her, and her expression faltered for a moment. She dragged herself back to the present, to what was happening now.

Nic knew he had to speak. Had no choice but to do so. He tried to think what to say and failed. Failed to do anything but let his eyes cling to her hungrily. If even a fragment of his mind was registering that she was gowned in haute couture, her hair dressed high on her head in convoluted coils and her throat emblazoned with an ornate sapphire necklace—a look utterly at odds with the casually styled way she'd been in the USA—he shook it aside.

Only her beauty mattered, and in that she was radiant. As beautiful as ever.

How could I have let her go? I must have been crazy to let her go!

The words leapt in his head, knocking down all the principles he lived his life by. His mind was ragged, but he had to force himself to find words to answer her.

'I—it's—complicated.' His voice sounded terse as he urgently pulled a mask over his expression, trying to pull together his thoughts, trying to work out how to handle this, how to cope with what was inevitably going to happen.

She was going to discover that, no, he was *not* working here at the Viscari St James's...

He saw her react to his blank expression, saw the withdrawal in her face as she backed away slightly.

'Oh, I'm sorry.' Fran halted. The leap that her heart had taken collapsed.

Belatedly she realised that if Nic were indeed working here at the Viscari in London, then maybe he shouldn't be mingling with the guests. Maybe the easy-going atmosphere at the Falcone Nevada did not prevail here at the Viscari. Maybe he was still on approval only, had to be cautious. Maybe he was supposed to be low-profile, here to keep an eye out for the security of guests who, like her, glittered with jewels at this gala event. Maybe—

Maybe you are the last person he wants to see—maybe that's why he's not exactly opening his arms to you.

Brutally, she reminded herself of what she'd said to herself often enough in the months since their road trip.

He's had every chance to get back in touch if he wanted to. He knows where you worked, where you lived, and could easily have found out you'd moved to Cambridge. He could easily have looked you up now that he's come over to the UK. But he didn't. So what does that tell you?

The answer was stark. It told her that he wasn't interested in her any more.

With that same hollowing inside her she watched the woman in the red evening dress come up to them. The woman was beautiful, and Fran felt it like a blow. Nic had moved on.

She felt emotion churn within her, shocking her with its power—a power it should not have, but did. Then, out of nowhere, the emotion was wiped away. Another took its place.

The beautiful brunette was lightly touching Nic's sleeve, her voice diffident. 'Would you excuse me for a few moments, Mr Falcone? I've just seen someone I should speak to...'

Her words wiped everything from Fran's hectic brain. She heard her own intake of breath sharply.

Then, the word *'What?'* broke from her like a gunshot.

What had that woman just called him? Mr *Falcone?* She couldn't have.

CHAPTER FIVE

FRAN'S FEATURES FROZE, her eyes widening in disbelief.

As if in slow motion, Nic moved. Took Lorna's arm from his sleeve. Nodded in dismissal, his face thunderous.

For a second longer Fran's eyes stayed blankly on the woman as she smiled her thanks uncertainly and then hurried away, as if sensing some untoward incident had just occurred and she wanted to be out of it.

Then Fran's eyes slewed back to Nic. There was a drumming in her ears, a blankness in her head. She stared at Nic. His face was masked, as if a steel screen had been slammed down over it. The face that was as familiar to her as her own. Nic's face.

Nic. Nic Rossi. Who worked in Security at the Falcone Nevada.

Mr Falcone.

It can't be—I misheard. I must have misheard.

'Tell me I misheard.' She spoke aloud, her voice as hollow as the gaping hole inside her.

She saw him give a quick, unmistakable, unarguable shake of his head, felt that wash of disbelief go through her again as he did so.

'No, you didn't,' he said. His voice sounded curt. 'I'm Nicolo Falcone.'

She stared, not taking it in. 'You said your name was Nic Rossi.' Her voice was hollow.

'It is,' he said. 'That's my birth name. I took the name Falcone when I decided to make something of myself.'

She took a step backwards, not realising that she had. It was an instinctive gesture—a withdrawal. Emotion was pounding within her, drumming in her ears.

'Why lie to me?' Her voice was a blade, accusing him.

Emotion flashed in his eyes. Those blue, blue eyes she had gazed into so often, for so long—eyes that crinkled at the corners when he laughed, that changed from laughter to desire, to hot, burning passion.

'I didn't lie. I just didn't tell you.'

His voice seemed to be coming from very far away. As if the man she knew was receding from her. Because the man she'd thought she knew didn't exist.

I thought he was one person, but he's another.

The hollowness was spreading. It was as if her whole being were now nothing but a shell, surrounding an emptiness that was yawning inside her. Then, suddenly, she saw his expression change, his eyes snap past her. She heard footsteps, then a voice. Deep. Commanding. Speaking in Italian.

'Francesca, are you all right?'

It was Cesare. Cesare was moving to her side, being very much the imperious Il Conte, throwing the aura of his protection around her, casting an inquisitorial look towards the man opposite her that kept him at a distance, that wanted to know why he was importuning her.

Instinctively—because Cesare was an old friend, because she'd known him all her life, because once she'd thought to live her life with him—Fran clutched at his arm, leaning her weight on it, which he supported instantly.

She said his name, faintly. 'Cesare...'

She saw that Nic heard it—Nic, the fabulously rich billionaire who owned the hotel she'd stayed in for the conference—owned that hotel, owned dozens more.

But not, as it happened, this one. For right now someone else was approaching them. Vito Viscari was stepping up beside her on her other side, flanking her just as Cesare was, throwing his protection around her as well. But the focus of his attention was on Nic.

'Falcone.' The voice was tight, borderline hostile.

She saw Nic's head turn. Nod. His mouth was set, his eyes steeled suddenly, acknowledging the presence of the man whose hotel this was. She heard Vito Viscari continue, in that same chill, tight tone of voice.

'I don't recall your name being on the invitation list, Falcone.' He, too, spoke in Italian—the language they all shared.

Fran saw Nic's mouth curl. 'That didn't prove necessary.'

'With you, what else should I expect?' There was a twist in Vito's voice. Then, with studied coolness, he challenged, 'So, have you come to admire? Or dismiss?'

'To assess,' came Nic's answer, his voice deeper than Vito's but just as clipped.

'And what is your assessment, Falcone?' Vito's eyes were unreadable. But Fran was dimly aware it was a taunt.

Nic gave a slow nod. 'Impressive,' he said— as if he begrudged the compliment but would not demean himself by denying it.

Vito tilted an eyebrow. 'Good of you,' he said sardonically.

The stand-off between them was palpable, and then dimly, through the frozen blankness that was the inside of her head, Fran became aware that someone else was joining them. Harry, her cousin, was sauntering up to them with all the casual self-assurance of someone who had been born an earl and would one day be a marquess and then a duke—a youth who had an entrée everywhere, however exclusive. The kind of inherent self-assurance that came with five hundred years of being bred to it.

'Hi,' he said cheerfully, in his upper-class public schoolboy accent, speaking English, utterly oblivious of the net of tension in the frozen tableau. 'Fantastic bash, this, Vito,' he said with a grin, raising his glass to his host. Then his gaze widened to throw an enquiring glance at the man opposite.

Stiffly, as if jolted into social niceties, Vito spoke. 'Falcone, allow me to introduce you to my guests...' There was a slightest emphasis on the word 'guests', as if to indicate that his rival was not one.

'Lord Cranleigh...' He nodded towards Harry, who waved his champagne glass airily as Vito continued, in English, his voice as tight as his expression. 'Il Conte di Mantegna you will obviously know of—have you met before? Perhaps not...' he said dismissively.

His expression changed very slightly, his eyes suddenly speculative, and he threw the briefest glance towards Fran, in the same protective manner Cesare had used.

'Though it would seem you have already made the acquaintance of Lord Cranleigh's cousin—Il Marchese d'Arromento's daughter, Donna Francesca di Ristori.'

It was as if slow motion had stilled to nothing. Most of all in Fran's hollowed brain. Then, as if motion had started again, she saw Nic's expression change. Saw it drain, stiffen. The steel mask dropped down over it again. Yet behind it she could see the glitter of his eyes.

She heard him speak.

'Donna... Francesca.'

The simple repetition. Two words. Like stones dropped from a great height, one after another. Then his eyes went past her to the man she was clinging to as if for dear life. The man she had called Cesare.

Cesare the hick...the country bumpkin. The farm boy. The dismissive names he'd given to the man who'd been in Fran's past paraded through his head with mocking brutality.

Cesare was the Count of Mantegna. Polished, cosmopolitan, a man of the world, owner of vast ancestral estates, moving in the very highest echelons of Roman society, holder of a title that stretched back a thousand years.

This...*this* was the man she'd spoken of that day, in another world, another life, when she'd sat beside him in that speedboat on the desert lake... The woman he'd romanced across the Canyonlands and deserts, in the wild, wide-open spaces of America, who'd laughed with him, travelled with him, made love with him...

His mouth twisted. His guts twisted.

I thought I knew who she was! Doc Fran, who gazed up at the stars and told me all about them. Who fell into my arms and held me close. Doc Fran, who didn't care that she was romancing a guy she took to be a security guard at a hotel.

But she wasn't that person at all. She came from a world that was nowhere like the free and easy democratic society of the States. Her world—her *true* world—was one of stiff formality and ancient titles, of blood that had been blue for centuries. A world of *palazzos* and *castellos*, of ancestors reaching back into the annals of history. A world of those born to privilege and possessions. A world that had nothing, *nothing* to do with him.

That never could. Nor anyone who belonged to it.

For one endless moment his gaze rested on her, then on the men standing in a protective rank beside her, flanking her, guarding her, keeping him at bay, keeping him away from her. The men she belonged to, in the world she came from, as she stood there in her couture gown, antique sapphires glittering in her priceless necklace... Donna Francesca...

Not the woman he knew. Had thought he knew...

But he hadn't. Not at all.

He turned away, feeling skewered, eviscerated. Walked off. Not caring that he was doing so. His stride was rapid, mechanical, and he almost pushed past other guests to reach the conservatory, march up to the elevator, jab at the button to open the doors, walk inside.

His face was a steel mask, his eyes glittering with an emotion he would not name.

But he knew what it was, and why it was scything through him like a knife in his guts.

'Nic, wait!'

A hand had seized the closing doors, forcing them open again. Fran stumbled inside, the tightness of her gown constricting her, her high heels twisting her ankles in her desperate haste. She grabbed the handrail to steady herself, hearing the doors slice shut again, felt the lift begin to descend.

'Nic—' She started again, but he cut across her. His voice hard.

'We have nothing to say to each other.' The words fell into the yawning space between them. Then, with a savage punctiliousness, he added, *'Donna Francesca.'*

Her face contorted. 'Don't call me that!'

The glitter in his eyes flashed, as coruscating as the priceless antique sapphires around her throat.

'But it is who you are,' he said. His voice was still harsh, biting out the words.

'So *what*?' she shot back.

Emotion was storming inside her. What had happened back there had been horrendous: Cesare at his most pompous and lordly, Harry being a Hooray Henry to a T, Vito barely civil and deliberately, she was sure, hammering home her family and her title. It was the very worst way she could have imagined Nic learning who she really was.

But he isn't 'just' Nic Rossi, either!

That fact seared across her.

'And Nicolo Falcone is who *you* are!' She took a shuddering breath. 'You never mentioned that, did you? And I never mentioned a title that means absolutely *nothing* in America!'

She saw his mouth tighten. 'But we are in Europe now, and you are Donna Francesca— as Viscari so *kindly* pointed out to me.'

Fran's eyes flashed. 'Well, that's what Vito knows me as! His step-cousin married Cesare—the man I turned down!'

'Ah, yes.' Nic's voice was tightly vicious, but the target was himself, for having once written off one of the leaders of Italian high society as a rustic farm boy. 'His Excellency the Count of Mantegna, no less!'

'Yes, and what of it?' she demanded. 'He's a family friend. I've known him since I was a child!'

Nic's eyes hardened. Of *course* the illustrious Count was a family friend. And a childhood one at that. What else should he be? They all knew each other, these aristos—knew each other and stuck together, protecting their privileges, protecting each other.

Memory daggered him. Just as the likes of Vito Viscari all protected their privileges—privileges they hadn't had to work for, had had handed to them on a plate. Effortlessly taking it as nothing more than their due, their God-given right. Not caring if it shut out those who'd actually had to *work* for everything they'd achieved.

Well, he wanted nothing to do with such people. Nothing to do with a woman who turned
out to be part of all that.

She's not the woman I thought she was.

The knowledge seared across him like a
burning brand.

'Donna Francesca, your family and your
friends are no concern of mine!' he ground
out. Savage anger was still scything across his
brain, rage at himself, at her…

Something contorted in her face. 'Nic, don't
be like this!'

Her hand reached towards him, as if to touch
him as she had touched him so often in their
time together. But now it faltered, unsure, uncertain. He was holding her at bay. Repelling
and repudiating her. And all that they had once
been to each other—

Memory scythed across her mind of how
they had stood together in an elevator that evening after the Sunset Drive and she had wondered whether he would kiss her, whether she
would kiss him back. That had been the very
start of their time together, their coming to-

gether in shared desire, becoming friends, then lovers.

How could this stone-faced, harsh-featured man holding her so coldly at bay be that same man?

She almost cried out with the anguish of it, of the clash of worlds between then and now.

He wasn't answering her impassioned plea, was shutting her out. His face was shuttered and closed. Blanking her. The elevator had stopped, had reached the lobby, and the doors were starting to open. He was ignoring her, turning towards them to exit the lift.

She would not chase him across the hotel. Before he moved she impulsively jabbed at the control buttons and the doors juddered shut again, the lift soaring upwards once more.

Nic gave what seemed to be a snarl of anger at her high-handedness. He turned on her. He wanted an end to this. Emotions were knifing through him, out of his control.

'Enough!'

A hand slashed into the air and suddenly, as Fran stared at him, consternation at what was happening, why it was happening, filling her, she saw him change. She had known

right from the first moment of their encounter
that he was tough, but it had been a toughness
that had never been directed at her. Now, suddenly, it was.

And it was a toughness that went way beyond
that required of a guy who worked in security
at a luxury casino hotel.

A hard, arctic gaze pinioned her. Suddenly
this was not Nic Rossi the man she knew, the
man she had spent such an easy-going, passionate, unforgettable time with. It was Nicolo
Falcone, billionaire owner of a global hotel
chain, with thousands of staff at his command,
a property portfolio that stretched around the
world, revenues that dwarfed anything her father possessed. Nicolo Falcone, who'd made
his immense fortune by his own efforts, starting from nothing, clawing his way to wealth
by strength of will.

And men like that were ruthless, single-
minded and not to be messed with.

Nor was he.

His hand lowered to the control panel, pressing the halt button, staying the elevator where
it was. Then he spoke.

'Donna Francesca,' he began, with an icy formality that chilled her to the quick as she stood staring at him, skewered by the arctic gaze of this man who was nothing like the man she'd thought she knew. 'You will oblige me by not attempting to delay my departure. You will also oblige me—' his mouth hardened even more as he issued not a request but an order, a warning '—by not attempting any further contact with me.'

The hand at the control panel pressed another button and the doors slid open on an intermediate floor.

'Goodnight, Donna Francesca.'

He stood, pointedly waiting for her to step out. She was staring at him, her face pinched. Defeated. Emotion bit in him, like acid, but he blanked it. Then, with a sudden sweep of her skirts, she walked out, holding herself as stiffly as if she were made of marble.

For a second—an endless second that seemed to stretch like the distance of the deserted corridor—Nic went on holding the door open. Then, numbly, he released the button, pressed for the lobby again, felt the elevator start its plummeting descent with a lurch. Leaving his guts somewhere way above.

Gaining the lobby, he walked out of the hotel, out on to the pavement. He didn't want to summon his car. Striding blindly, he headed towards Mayfair, his face still a steel mask. That same emotion still acid in his mouth.

Blindly, Fran reached the end of the corridor, pushed open the doors leading to the stairwell. She had to return to the party—a lifetime of training that told her one could not indulge one's feelings at the expense of social demands impelled her. Yet emotions were tumbling through her, jarring and clashing. To see Nic again…to learn who he really was without warning, so abruptly…and he to learn her other identity, equally without warning—

Was it just shock? Mutual shock on both their parts?

But he'd seemed so *angry* to discover she was Donna Francesca.

I'm not angry that he's really Nicolo Falcone! In fact—

She stopped, as she was climbing the stairs to the roof level. If Nic really was Nicolo Falcone then surely that was *good*, wasn't it? Wasn't it good that she was Donna Francesca as well as

Doc Fran? Wasn't it *better* that Nic was Nicolo Falcone? Not Nic Rossi working in Security in a hotel in Nevada?

Because if she were Donna Francesca, and he was Nicolo Falcone, then—

Her thoughts raced through her head as she painstakingly climbed upwards. Whatever the shock that had followed after that brunette had disclosed his real identify, nothing could take away from her that rush of emotion she'd felt, overpowering her when she had seen him.

Joy.

She felt it again—felt that surge of pleasure and delight at seeing him once more. Felt the rush that came with it, the lift of her spirits.

Telling herself that Nic was in the past, that her time with him was over, was totally useless. She felt emotion sweep within her yet again—and hit a wall.

She jerked to a halt, lungs tightening. That brunette...

Her insides hollowed. Nic—whether he was Nic Rossi or Nicolo Falcone didn't matter—had moved on. That was why he was repudiating her, rejecting her.

Bleakness filled her. Slowly she resumed her

heavy climb. That was the reason—the obvious, glaring reason—Nic would have nothing to do with her.

He had someone else, and whether she was Doc Fran or Donna Francesca made no difference at all to him.

It was the only explanation.

And it devastated her.

'Vito!' Eloise Viscari exclaimed, coming up to her husband. 'Is it true? Did Nicolo Falcone really have the nerve to turn up here tonight?'

Instantly Fran tensed at the name. The rooftop party had finally ended, but she and Harry, together with Cesare and Carla, had been invited by Vito to join him and Eloise, who was heavily pregnant with their second child, and so hadn't attended the garden launch, for an informal supper in their private suite at the hotel.

Fran would have preferred not to go, but social obligations could not be avoided, however much her personal preference would have been otherwise.

As she heard Vito answer his wife, Fran was aware of Cesare glancing at her. Since rejoining the roof party she'd been aware of his watchful eyes on her. He knew her well enough to know when she was upset, however much she strove to conceal it. She did not want him asking questions why.

Not when she scarcely knew the answer herself.

'Yes, he came as Lorna Linhurst's plus-one,' Vito was confirming. His voice and mouth were tight.

'Well, she's either his latest squeeze in a long, long line of squeezes or she's touting for work at Falcone,' Eloise said caustically. 'Whichever, she won't get any more work from *you*, Vito!'

'Falcone?' Harry joined the conversation, strolling towards them from the buffet table where he'd been helping himself liberally. 'Is that the guy built like a forward you introduced to us? Guy with the broken nose? *Is* he a rugby player?' he asked casually.

'No,' Cesare corrected him. 'He owns the Falcone chain of hotels.'

'No way!' Harry commented cheerfully, putting away the last of a large slice of quiche. 'Looks a bit of a bruiser to me!'

'A good description in many ways,' Vito observed grimly. 'Especially in business.'

Harry looked questioningly at Vito, but it was Carla who answered. 'Last year he briefly acquired half the entire Viscari portfolio in a highly hostile corporate raid. It came to nothing in the end, but it was pretty nasty at the time.' Her tone changed, sounding chastened. 'It was all my fault—I should have stopped my mother, Vito's step-aunt, selling her shares to him.'

Eloise reached a hand across to her. 'Carla—no. Don't go there. It's all sorted now.' Her voice was sympathetic.

'Only because *your* mother bought the hotels back for Vito from Falcone's investors!' Carla exclaimed.

'Well, that's one of the plus points of having a mum who runs her very own hedge fund,' Eloise riposted lightly. 'And Falcone's talons are out of us now. We've seen him off! He's furious—but who cares?'

Fran was staring at them, totally focussed. *What* had they just been saying?

Then Eloise was continuing. 'Anyway, he's gone off on an acquisition spree instead. The most recent was in Nevada—not in Vegas, but some desert resort.'

Harry glanced to Fran. 'Sounds like where you went for that conference last summer. Tonio had to yank you back when Gramps had his heart attack.'

All eyes turned to Fran. With effort, though her thoughts were suddenly hectic, she kept her voice calm. 'Yes. It had only recently opened, I believe.'

'Any good?' Eloise asked enquiringly. She smiled. 'Just casing the opposition!'

'It was very luxurious,' Fran answered. 'Beautifully situated—right out in the desert. Amazing scenery.' Her voice was stilted, but she knew she had to sound as normal as possible. Yet in her head flashed the memory of her and Nic, on that first outing, watching the sun set in a blaze of gold.

She blinked, and the memory was gone.

Carla was speaking again. 'His latest venture is New York. He's finally found a Manhattan site of his own now that he can't have Vito's,' she said.

Eloise held up her hand. 'No more talk about Falcone—the wretched man or his hotels! Not a patch on Viscari!'

She raised her glass of orange juice, then

glanced to where her husband was talking in a low, preoccupied voice to Cesare.

'Darling, we're just about to toast your success tonight! Do pay attention!'

There was laughter, and they all raised their glasses to Vito. But as Fran lowered hers and the conversation turned general, she realised Cesare had come to stand beside her, where she sat on one of the sofas, trying to conceal her suddenly hectic thoughts.

He inclined his head to hers. 'Is that why Falcone approached you this evening? Had you encountered him in Nevada while you were there?' His voice was low, and he was speaking in Italian.

Fran swallowed. 'Briefly,' she acknowledged, her tone constrained. She did *not* want Cesare probing.

She saw Cesare's expression tighten. 'Then I hope, Francesca, that you will take this in the spirit with which I offer it. I was concerned when I saw you with him—which is why I came up. It is a concern shared by Vito, who knows his reputation—as he was just telling me.' He paused a moment. 'Nicolo Falcone is well known as a womaniser, so—'

Fran cut across him repressively. 'Cesare, I appreciate what you're saying, but—'

He smiled faintly. 'Yes, I know—it's none of my business. But we go back a long way, you and I, so I will claim the privilege of speaking now in a fraternal way. I would not like to see you misled by someone of...let us say, an unscrupulous disposition. So, if Falcone was importuning you tonight—'

She shook her head decisively. Any 'importuning' had come from her, she thought bleakly, when she had demanded he speak to her...talk to her...

'I was surprised to see him here, that was all,' she said constrainedly. 'As, apparently, was everyone else.' She frowned, putting into words what was uppermost in her head right now. 'I hadn't realised he'd tried to take over Viscari and lost.'

'It was headline news in the financial press in Italy, but you were in the States at the time,' Cesare said. 'There's huge friction between Falcone and Viscari.'

She was relieved she had no opportunity to reply. Harry had sauntered over to them, demolishing a chicken leg as he did so.

'Fran, old bean, I'm off clubbing. You've got keys for the flat, haven't you?'

She nodded. Most of the family made use of Harry's father's flat in Chelsea when they were in town. Restlessly, she got to her feet. Her thoughts were still hectic, emotions racing. What had been disclosed just now was fuelling them. She wanted to be gone.

Using the excuse of Harry's departure, she took her leave. It seemed ages before she was in the chauffeured hotel car Vito had ordered for her, dropping Harry off to meet up with his friends. Alone at last, she felt her mind race, replaying everything she'd heard said in Vito's suite.

Was *that* why Nic had been so icily hostile to her? Because she'd been Vito Viscari's guest? Because he'd aligned her with the man who was his bitter rival in business? Add to that the fact that she was the last person he'd wanted to meet up with again, that he'd thought her safely tucked away back on the West Coast, never to be encountered again now that he had moved on to another woman in his life...

Something knotted inside her, and with a smothered cry she released the pent-up emotions that she had bottled up inside her all evening since that disastrous encounter on the rooftop—that wretched, icy exchange when she'd run after him. How could it have come to this? That Nic—*Nic*—who'd swept her up into his arms, laughed with her, made love to her, driven across deserts with her, should be so harsh towards her now?

Oh, their affair might be over, and he might have moved on, but everything in her—every feeling—was rebelling at letting that cold, callous scene between them be all that was left between them now.

We parted as friends. I don't want to remember him like this, now, the way he was this evening.

Hands twisting in her lap, she stared blindly out of the car's front window as it made the turn into a large square in Mayfair, en route for Chelsea. She suddenly started. Above the white pillared entrance to the building that dominated one side of the square a blue flag hung, illuminated by skilful lighting. A gold falcon on a blue field—

'Stop the car!'

The driver pulled up at the kerb. From there

she could see the gold lettering above the grand doorway. *Falcone Mayfair.*

She swallowed, aware the driver was waiting for further instructions. Aware of much more than that. Of an urge she could not stop. An urge that was pressing on her like a sudden impulse she must obey.

To be passing the Falcone hotel just like this, unexpectedly… It was a sign, surely? A sign to do what was leaping in her head.

I have to do this. I can't leave it the way he left it. I won't let him spoil my memories of that time we had.

With fast-beating heart she dismissed the car, went into the hotel. Though she had no idea if Nic were here at the moment, she could but ask. Try and find out where he was if he wasn't here.

Straightening her spine, she sailed up to Reception as if she owned the world. Sometimes being Donna Francesca, granddaughter of the Duke of Revinscourt, resplendent in her couture gown and her antique sapphires, could come in useful. It would now—she would make sure of it.

'Good evening,' she said, her smile polite

but supremely expectant of being paid attention to. 'Can you tell me if Mr Falcone is back yet? We were together earlier this evening and arranged to meet here later.'

The receptionist was co-operative, but cautious. 'I believe so, madam, but let me check.'

She picked up a phone. 'Ah, Mr Falcone, there is someone in Reception for you.' The woman glanced expectantly at Fran, waiting for a name.

Fran smiled. Her heart was thumping in agitation, but she did not let it show.

'Lorna Linhurst,' she said serenely.

CHAPTER SIX

NIC SAT AT his desk in his residence, trying to concentrate on the latest occupancy figures on his screen and failing. There was only one focus for his thoughts—one he did not want to have but which burned in his head, flaring on his retinas as if she stood there still in front of him the way she had that evening, suddenly reappearing in his life. Vividly real and as beautiful as ever.

With an oath, he pushed his chair back, gazed grimly across the sitting room. His residence was on the topmost floor, with slanting eaves, set into what had once been the servants' quarters of the Georgian mansion. Maybe there were those who thought it a fitting place for him.

His mouth twisted. Well, now he owned the whole damn mansion—and dozens more multi-million-dollar properties. Not bad for a slum kid! A slum kid who'd somehow 'made the acquaintance'—Viscari's supercilious words seemed to mock him savagely—of the daughter of a *marchese*.

Donna Francesca.

The name, her courtesy title, was hardly used any more, but still it was redolent of centuries of fine breeding, of titles and lands and privileges, and coats of arms and ancient houses and historic *palazzos* filled with priceless artworks—all related to each other, all marrying each other, all closing ranks against outsiders, all helping each other to keep their privileges for themselves.

Oh, Italy might be a republic these days—most European countries were—but that didn't mean a thing to those born to the aristocracy. Maybe they didn't call the shots politically any longer, but they had the rest of the world handed to them on a plate.

They'd worked for none of it—had simply sat back and inherited it. Just the way Vito Viscari had sat back and waited for his plush inheritance to fall into his lap, courtesy of his father and uncle, who'd ensured he'd had his path to the top smoothed and eased, had never had to strive for anything. Brushing aside as irrelevant anyone who got in the way—as he had been brushed aside in favour of the pampered young Viscari heir.

Scorn filled him—a familiar scorn that reached to the woman who'd stood in front of him this evening, a woman from that gilded world of privilege and aristocracy. And another emotion was shafting through it—anger. Anger that she wasn't who he'd thought she was.

I thought she was Dr Fran Ristori—with her golden hair and a smile to take the breath out of my body. And a body to fuse to mine like it was part of me.

Memory, hot and searing, tore at him.

To think he'd even contemplated breaking his rule of a lifetime to get back in touch with her. To seek to capture again that time he'd had with her. His expression hardened. Thank God he hadn't! Thank God he'd done what he'd done all his life—moved on.

Whoever the hell she really was, he was done with her. So why should he care that she was the daughter of a *marchese*?

The phone on his desk was ringing and he snatched it up.

'Yes?'

His voice was curt. Who wanted him at this late hour of the evening? He was in no mood to be hospitable. Then, as the receptionist gave the name of his unexpected visitor, his frown cleared. Unexpected she might be, but he should make the most of it.

Hadn't he been telling himself he'd moved on? Well… His expression changed again. Now he really could. This very evening. Right away. Whatever had brought Lorna here, he would take advantage of it. He would open champagne, make it clear to her that he was interested in more than her skills in garden design and see where it took them.

He wanted her to say yes.

Memory, unwanted but piercing, arrowed through him. Once it had been another woman, with golden hair and a beauty to inflame him, he'd wanted to say yes.

Enough! The same word that he'd silenced her with sliced through his brain now.

'Tell Ms Linhurst,' he said to the receptionist, making his voice far less curt, 'that she is most welcome.'

He hung up. Strode to the climate-controlled drinks cabinet, drawing out a suitable bottle

of champagne, setting out two flutes beside
it, checking that the lighting created the right
ambience for the message he wished to convey
to the woman who was going to be his way to
move on from the woman he needed to move
on from…

There was a soft rap at the door. He crossed
towards it, opened it with a welcoming smile.

'Lorna, this is a most pleasant surprise—'
he began warmly.

Then the welcoming smile was wiped from
his face.

Fran was inside the door before Nic could register it or stop her.

'What the hell…?'

There was nothing welcoming in his voice
now, nothing warm.

She strode past him, the long silk skirts of
her gown swishing. 'Nic, I have to talk to you!'
She slewed round to face him, and as she did so
she was burningly conscious of his raw physical presence all over again.

He was still in his tuxedo, but his top shirt
button was undone, the black bow tie hang-
ing open either side. In the hours since she'd

set eyes on him his jaw had shadowed with the beginning of regrowth, and it gave him a rough, piratical edge that hollowed something out inside her.

How often in their time together, lolling in bed together late at night, or early in the morning, had she run her fingers along that roughened edge, glorying in the sheer masculinity of it until he caught her fingers, hauled her mouth to his and started all over again in his urgent, demanding possession of her?

A word in Italian escaped from him, a crudity that broke on the air, and she blenched. Nic didn't care that she could understand it—all that was in him now was an open anger that was instantaneous. There was shock too—and more than shock.

Her image had been burning in his head and now it was more than just that. It was *her*—her presence—just as it had been on the rooftop of the Viscari. As resplendent as it had been then. And he realised there was no way he could move on with Lorna.

His eyes honed in on the couture gown in blue silk, the sapphires snaked around her pale throat, the golden hair piled high on her head.

La Donna Francesca in all her aristocratic grandeur.

Then her words registered with him. *I have to talk to you!*

Anger slashed across his consciousness. No, she did *not* have to talk to him! He wanted none of it.

His expression closed. Hardened. The way it had in the elevator. 'There is nothing I wish to hear, Donna Francesca—' he began, his voice cold.

Something flashed in her eyes, and he realised with a start that it was anger too.

'Well, tough, Nic—because you're going to hear it! I will *not* be treated like this by you!'

It was the wrong thing to say. Immediately his eyes narrowed, his voice icing. 'Do *not* throw your aristocratic privileges at *me*, because they don't impress me! God knows how you blagged your way in here. But you can leave right now!'

He made to go and open the door, but Fran was there before him.

'Nic, *no!*' Her voice changed and she took a heaving breath. Emotion was storming in her, threatening to overwhelm her. She'd nerved herself for this and she would see it through. She *must*.

'Nic, *listen* to me. You've got no business stonewalling me like this. It's *me*, Fran. You owe me some courtesy, at least. I've not done any harm to you. Listen...' She took another shuddering breath. 'Don't take your anger out on me! I am not anything to do with whatever the hell is going on between you and Vito. I didn't even *know* you'd tried to take over half his company, let alone that it was ripped back from you. Why should I? I didn't even damn well know you were Nicolo Falcone. You made sure I didn't know.'

Nic's voice stayed icy. 'And *you* made sure I didn't know who *you* really were!'

'Because it wasn't relevant!' she shot back vehemently. 'It wasn't relevant then, and it isn't now.' She took another shuddering breath. Held out her hand towards him. 'Nic, please, don't be like this.' Her voice changed, dropped. 'There was something good between us...don't spoil it now! Don't spoil those memories—'

She broke off, feeling emotion rising in her, her hand still outstretched towards him, where he stood rigid and unmoving.

But behind the mask of his face something was moving. Something was building like an unstoppable tide. She was standing there, breasts heaving, the jewels around her throat catching the low lamplight. The woman he was finally going to put behind him. Into the past, where she needed to be. Needed to stay. The past that was reaching forward now, reaching towards him as she was reaching her hand towards him, her eyes huge, lips parted, as if imploring him. As if tempting him beyond endurance.

'There was something *good*, Nic, and it doesn't deserve your hostility to me!'

Something changed in his eyes. Something that glittered with memory and was fuelled by the heat suddenly rising in his body, the heat *she* was engendering, with her slender body moulded by that gown that showed every curve, every contour, the body he knew with all the intimacy of possession.

As if of their own volition his feet took a step towards her. He did not touch her outstretched hand. Instead his fingers reached to touch her cheek. Lightly…the slightest brush.

'Shall I tell you what there was between us? Shall I show you?'

The fingers trailed to her lips, grazed their outline. The husk in his voice was low, sensual...

She stilled. 'Nic, *no*! I didn't come here because—' She broke off, stricken. Lifted her hand to push his fingers away. 'Nic, I know you have someone else in your life now—another woman! I *know* what we had is over.'

A rasp broke from him and there was a glitter in his eyes now, like the glitter of light on the sapphires around her throat.

'There *is* no other woman...' The words fell from his lips, hoarse.

How could there be any other woman when *this* woman had reappeared in his life, out of nowhere, taking his senses by storm? As she had the very first time he'd laid eyes on her.

As she always would...every time...

The truth seared through him like a burning brand. He would *always* want her, this woman he could not resist. He would be foolish to think otherwise.

He saw her expression change at what he'd

said, heard the intake of her breath, saw her pupils start to dilate, a flush rise in her cheeks, her breasts rise and fall. Her hand fell to her side, too weak to ward him off as he lifted his fingers to her cheek again, slid his hand around the delicate line of her jaw to cup the nape of her neck, drawing her towards him.

She faltered, and yielded, exhaling his name in a breath, on a soft, helpless sigh, as his other hand reached forward towards her straining breasts, curved openly around one lush mound, felt it crest through the silk.

Desire shot through him. Hot, urgent. The world receded, ceased to exist. He heard her gasp—a gasp he knew, recognised. It was a gasp of pleasure, of arousal.

'Nic...' Her voice was a low moan, an exhalation of desire.

He moved towards her. 'Shall I show you what there was between us?' he said again, and his voice was that low husk still, his lashes dropping over his eyes, mouth lowering to hers.

His kiss was velvet. Slow, deliberate, controlled, opening her mouth to his with practised ease. A moan broke from her. A cry inside her head. This should not be happening—it was not why she had come.

But she was beyond stopping him. Beyond anything except letting her clutch bag tumble to the floor to free both her hands, sliding them around the strong column of his body, feeling a release inside her as she did so, as she felt the warmth of his body beneath her sliding palms.

She said his name again and it was a sigh, a plea.

A yielding.

She could not stand against it—against what was happening. She hadn't come here for this... She had come for understanding, for making peace, for—

I came for this.

The truth—the truth she'd blinded herself to—seared across her brain.

'Oh, God, Nic... *Nic!*' It was half a sob, half a sigh, and then she was kissing him back, kissing him with a fervour, an urgency that was like a flame lit within her, a flame that was becoming a fire—hot, unstoppable, consuming everything, consuming all the world.

Everything ceased to exist. There was only

this, only Nic, only his mouth on hers, his hands on her, and hers crushing him to her, his stance shifting so that she was cradled against his hard, lean hips. He wanted her. He wanted her with all the urgency with which she wanted him.

Hunger leapt in her. Her mind was a daze, a jumble of naked, desperate desire.

Nic—only Nic! Nic, who was sweeping her up into his arms as if she weighed as much as a feather, who was striding with her to another room, lowering her down upon a bed, coming down beside her. His mouth fusing with hers again.

Words came from him as he drew breath, but he did not know what. Knew only that he could not draw back. That all he wanted was here, now. With her. With Fran. Clothes were in the way—impossible, unnecessary. Must be cast aside somehow, anyhow.

Urgency filled him, drove him onwards. Somewhere in the last recesses of his sanity he knew that this was mad, insane. That this was the last thing he should be doing. But rational thought was gone, burned away completely as he found her naked body waiting for him, her eyes wide, pupils dilated, gaze blind with passion and desire.

A passion and desire that was blinding him too…

He could not resist her, and nor did he want to. He wanted only to sink himself within her, to have her body opening to his, claiming him, taking him in.

And with a cry of triumph she was his possession and he was hers. She cried out too, her legs wrapping herself around him so he could not escape.

Not until the great tide sweeping up in him—overpowering, unstoppable, gaining power as it swept, taking him over—broke in a shuddering, low-throated roar that went on and on.

He could hear the echo in her voice crying out, felt her whole body clenching around him, convulsing with cry after cry, endless and infinite, it seemed, until, after an eternity he felt his body start to slacken, and hers, the tide ebbing from him, from her, her limbs falling exhausted to the sheets, his shoulders lowering, meeting hers, folding her into him so that the frantic pounding of their hearts was pressed, one to the other, their sweating bodies fused together, collapsing into each other, breaths ragged, exhausted.

He said her name. Slurred, inchoate. Then wrapped her to him, feeling a sweeping lassitude taking him over, impossible to halt. Impossible to do anything other than say her name again and let his eyes fall shut, let sleep—post-coital, exhausted—consume him.

With Fran in his arms. The only place he wanted her…

Fran stirred. Her limbs were heavy. She moved them slowly across the fine cotton sheets. Seeking… Seeking Nic's warm, embracing body.

But he wasn't there.

Her eyes sprang open, blind for a second, then they adapted. Letting her see the bright outline of the doorway and Nic framed within it. He was wearing a white towelling robe and was quite motionless. Then he spoke.

'You need to go,' he said. He reached out with his hand, flicked a switch on the wall so that twin bedside lights came on. 'You need to go,' he said again.

She stared. There was something wrong with his face. It was as if it was carved in stone.

Hands plunged into the pockets of the towelling robe, he stood four-square—immobile. She saw him take a breath, steel himself visibly.

'What just happened should not have,' he said. 'It was...' he breathed out '...a mistake.'

She could feel her heart start to beat faster within her body, with heavy slugs. It was all she could feel. Nothing else...nothing at all. There seemed to be a wall inside her, somewhere around her skull. Keeping her together. It was all that was keeping her together.

He took another breath. 'I'll leave you to dress. A car will take you wherever you need to go.'

He turned away. In her head, a cry came—his name, just his name. But she did not give it voice. Could not. Would not. She would do nothing except ease her body from the bed, find her underwear, scattered somewhere, her dress, and even her necklace, on the side table...

Somehow she dressed. Somehow she pinned up her hair, which had tumbled wantonly over her shoulders. Her hands were shaking, and still there was the same wall around her mind.

Still the hideous thumping of her heartbeat.
Marching her forward, into the sitting room.

Nic turned, his eyes on her. Eyes that were
blank. He bent to pick up her fallen evening
bag, handed it to her wordlessly. His face was
set, a nerve ticking at his jaw.

She took the bag, not letting her fingers
touch his, slithered her sapphire necklace into
it. Murmured a low 'thank you', not meeting
his eyes. She walked towards the door and he
opened it for her. Only there did she turn her
head briefly, so briefly. Her throat was as tight
as if barbed wire were around it.

'Goodbye, Nic.' There was no emotion in her
voice. She would not permit it. 'I won't trouble
you again. You have my word.'

Then she turned away, crossed to the elevator, its doors standing open, stepped inside.
The doors closed, and Nic was gone from sight.

Gone from her life.

Finally gone.

Behind her, Nic went on standing, motionless, staring at the closed doors of the elevator. He had sent her away. It was what he'd
wanted to do. Needed to do. Surfacing from
that post-coital slumber to the realisation of

what had happened had been like waking up with a punch to his guts. Slamming home to him just what he had done. The impossibility of it.

You need to go.

Go back to the world she came from, to the person she was—Donna Francesca, the person he wanted nothing to do with.

Nothing.

It was the only thing that made sense. Because sure as hell emotion scythed through him now, knifing in his eyes. Nothing else made sense. And not, above all, the sudden yawning emptiness inside him. That least of all.

CHAPTER SEVEN

FRAN WAS HURRYING past the majestic elevation of King's College Chapel, shivering in the chill east wind blowing up from the Backs. Was it the cold, or was she sickening for something? She hadn't felt right for over a week now.

Her thoughts hollowed. A bug was the last thing she cared about assailing her. Far, far worse was the desolation inside her.

How could I have let it happen? How could I have let myself? Let Nic?

Her thoughts sheered away, but their echo hung in her head like a weight she could not move. The clutch of nausea came again. She should have cancelled this luncheon engagement she was hurrying to, but it was too late now. Cesare would be waiting for her.

Still in the UK, he'd driven up to Cambridge with Carla, who was at the Fitzwilliam, interviewing an art specialist there, and had suggested he and Fran meet for lunch. Fran had found it hard to say no, yet she was deeply reluctant.

She was in no mood for socialising. No mood for anything except burying herself in her work, wanting only to immerse herself in it, block out everything else. Block every memory, especially the one that was trying to seek entrance—the one she must not allow entrance to.

Her mind sheered away again. She glanced across at the imposing frontage of the colleges, all so familiar. A sense of claustrophobia assailed her. Cambridge seemed to be closing in around her, and apart from her work she had no time for it any more. She no longer found the antiquity, the archaic traditions—from the meticulous formality of High Table to the endless rivalries between the colleges—as appealing as she had once found them, as an undergrad thrilled to be accepted into this ancient seat of learning, these hallowed halls. Since then she had spent too long in the USA, enjoying the freedom there.

Memory clutched at her again—of just what freedoms she had found in the States—and sheered away again. It had not been academic freedom she'd been remembering.

No, don't go there! Don't go anywhere at all except the present—today, now. Meeting Cesare for lunch, even though she didn't want to. Didn't want his shrewd gaze on her, seeing her agitation, wondering at the cause of it. Coming up with a reason for it.

Cesare was not an easy person to hide things from, and the last thing on earth she wanted was any replay of his warning to her about Nicolo Falcone.

The nausea came again, putting Cesare and her reluctance to meet him out of her mind, making her take a steadying breath that did not steady her. Her breasts felt tender, her abdomen distended. As if she were pre-menstrual…

She frowned, confused. Her cycle was regular, and PMS usually hit only a couple of days before her period, which wasn't due for a week. So why—?

She stopped dead. Her hand flew to her mouth, eyes widening in horror. No—no, it couldn't be! It just couldn't! Memory racked her—a memory she didn't want to have, but had to make herself have. That night that should never have happened!

He used protection! Dear God, he must have used protection! He must have!

But she could remember nothing—nothing except the white-out passion that had blinded her, consumed her.

A smothered cry broke from her. With a gasp, she started forward again, changing direction, plunging into the shopping area of Cambridge. Desperate to find a chemist.

How she got through the next two hours she didn't know. Somehow she coped with lunch. Cesare must have seen how distracted she was, but thankfully he made no observations on it, was his usual urbane self.

Only once, when she answered him at random, did he pause and ask if she was all right. She made a face, said she was coming down with a bug and changed the subject to something about how her mother and sister were in the throes of preparations for Adrietta's lavish engagement party—to which, of course, Cesare and Carla had been invited as family friends.

Then, at the end of the meal, as she was getting to her feet, Cesare drew back her chair for her. Her nerves totally on edge, she fumbled for her handbag, managing to knock it to the floor. It spilled open, and instantly she bent to retrieve the disgorged contents, exclaiming about her clumsiness, urgently stashing away the tell-tale item she'd purchased from the chemist on the way here, desperate to head home and use it.

Desperate to discover whether she was panicking unnecessarily.

'Francesca!' Cesare's voice was shocked.

She wheeled about, clutching her handbag to her chest as if to hide it from X-ray vision. But one look at Cesare's expression told her it was too late.

She threw her head up. 'It's none of your business, Ces!' she said furiously.

His face tautened, and she was sorry she had spoken so sharply.

She took a ragged breath. 'Yes, I know you're protective of me! You've said so before! And I've told you it isn't necessary!'

His dark eyes rested on her. 'If the test is positive are you going to tell him?'

He did not say *Falcone*, but she heard it all the same. She bit her lip, unable to reply, and into the silence Cesare spoke again.

'A father has a right to know, Francesca.'

She shut her eyes, anguished. 'Ces, *please*, I can't talk about this! I don't even know what the test will show.' There was a weariness in her now, that dragged her features into misery. 'All I know, believe me, is that if it is positive, it will not be welcome news to him.'

He did not reply, but his expression was grim as they left the restaurant. On the pavement he turned to her. 'A father,' he said, and there was a sternness in his voice that steeled his expression, 'also has an *obligation* to know—'

She cut across him, agitated, wanting only to stop this ordeal. 'There may not be anything *to* know! And this is *my* situation, for *me* to deal with. *If* there is anything to deal with at all.'

But within the hour, as she stared at the blue line forming on the small white stick, she knew, along with the numbness that was filling her whole body, her whole disbelieving mind, that there was, indeed, a situation for her to deal with.

* * *

Nic was back in Rome. The Manhattan launch had been a triumph, putting the latest, most glittering addition to the Falcone portfolio on the map. New money attracted new money. And if the Falcone Manhattan proved to be the last place old money wanted to be seen at—well, he wasn't interested in old money.

Or in those who had it.

His mouth tightened. No, not in anyone who had old money. Or titles just as old. Even if they came with blonde hair down to the waist and a beauty to light the night sky with.

No. The guillotine sliced down. Fran was out of his life. She had to stay out. Anything else was impossible.

I want nothing to do with anyone from her world—nothing.

He swore, pushing back his chair, striding to the window, gazing out at Rome blindly.

You have to forget her. You have to. You have to want to forget her...

The phone on his desk rang and he snatched it up. It was his PA.

'You have a visitor, Signor Falcone.' She spoke diffidently. 'He has no appointment, but...' her voice became even more diffident '...it is Il Conte di Mantegna...'

She trailed off.

Nic stilled.

'Show him in,' he said. He dropped the phone, thoughts racing. None of them good.

As the door opened, and his PA admitted his totally uninvited and unexpected visitor, Nic stood poised on the balls of his feet, perfectly balanced. With part of his mind he realised he was in a ready pose—the stance that every fighter took on just before the first blows lashed out.

Cesare di Mondave, Il Conte di Mantegna, who enjoyed an entrée everywhere in Rome—including, so it seemed, the HQ of Falcone International—walked in. The very way he walked put Nic's back up—as if the whole world belonged to him and always had.

'Falcone,' said Cesare, his eyes resting on Nic.

They were unreadable, and Nic kept his likewise.

'Signor Il Conte,' he returned. His voice was neutrally impassive. Eyes veiled. Watchful. Senses on high alert. Muscles primed.

A flicker of what might have passed for humour showed in the Conte's face. 'I'm not here to fight with you, Falcone,' he murmured. His eyes skimmed over Nic's face, as if trying to read him. 'You might want to sit down,' he said.

'Might I?' replied Nic, doing no such thing. Adrenaline, the kind before a fight, was sharp-set in him.

'Yes,' said Cesare and, uninvited, took possession of the chair in front of Nic's desk. Nic threw himself into his own chair, swinging it back to stare at Il Conte, his hands gripped over the arms. Muscles still tensed. What the hell *was* this?

He soon found out.

'I'm doing you the courtesy, Falcone,' he heard Cesare di Mondave say in cool, clipped tones, 'of assuming that you have absolutely no knowledge of what I am going to tell you.'

Nic's eyes narrowed. They were very blue. Very hard. 'Which is…?'

Dark, unreadable eyes rested on him, and Nic realised the man was steeling himself to speak.

A second later, he knew why.

'Are you aware, Falcone,' he heard Cesare di

Mondave ask, with sudden tension in the cool, clipped tones, 'that Francesca—' he took an intake of breath '—may be pregnant?'

The breath left Nic's lungs as if a vacuum had sucked it out of him in one gigantic inhalation.

'What?' The word shot from him, propelling his body forward so that he was pressing down on the arms of his chair.

'You don't deny the possibility?'

There was something in Cesare di Mondave's voice that registered in Nic and told him that he hadn't been sure of what he'd announced.

Nic's face hardened. Inside his head chaos had taken over. But his voice, as he spoke, was edged like a blade. 'Do you really imagine it is any of your business?'

Now it was Cesare's eyes that narrowed. 'Donna Francesca will *always* have my protection,' he bit out. 'Which is why I'm here.' His expression changed. 'So, now that you know, you can do what you are required to do.'

Chaos was still raging in Nic's head. But he couldn't pay it any attention—not right now. Right now his adrenaline was running and his opponent was in his sights.

'And what, Signor Il Conte di Mantegna, do

you think that is?' His hands had tightened over the chair arms—tightened with a deadly grip.

Then suddenly, moving with a lightning speed that Nic had not expected, Cesare was on his feet, the palms of his hands slammed down on the desk in front of Nic. Eyeballing him.

'If you need me to tell you, Falcone, then I'd sooner throw you out of the window right now! Leave you to the street dogs to eat!' He straightened. Looked down at Nic. 'You've got twenty-four hours before I tell her I've told you. She's in Rome today. At her parents' apartment.'

He walked out of the room. Behind him, at his desk, Nic very slowly sat back in his chair. The adrenaline had drained out of him. He hadn't the strength to move—not a muscle. In his head, the seething chaos suddenly was not there any more. In its place was only one thing. One emotion. One urgency.

He snapped his hand forward. Reached for his phone. 'I need an address immediately!' he bit out to his PA. 'The Rome residence of the Marchese d'Arromento. Right now!'

* * *

Fran was on her laptop, drafting her resignation to her professor. She could not continue at Cambridge, nor even stay in Europe at all. Urgency impelled her. Her mind was too distracted to think about work, which was why she'd come here, to her parents' Rome apartment, after the ordeal of attending Adrietta's lavish engagement party, where she'd forced herself to appear carefree for her sister and parents' sake.

But Cesare had been there too, with Carla, and grimly Fran had known that because she had not told him the pregnancy test had been negative he had realised that the opposite was true.

Instinctively, her hand glided to her stomach. There was nothing to indicate the profound, irreversible change that was happening in her. On the surface she looked just as she always had. It would take weeks for her pregnancy to show.

It's like starlight... taking light years to reach us. So long that some stars have burnt out by the time their light reaches us.

Her pregnancy would be like that—she would be long gone before it showed.

Emotion rippled through her. But eventually, like starlight, the baby would arrive. Arrive and have to be coped with, with all the implications thereof. And the first, overwhelming implication was the one that she had known right from the very beginning.

I can't tell him. I can't. It doesn't matter what Cesare said. Nic couldn't have made it clearer that he wants nothing to do with me.

No, she could not tell him.

Heaviness, as if there were a weight crushing her, pressed down upon her. All she could do was what she was doing. What she was going to *have* to do. To go as far away as she could, make a new life for herself and her baby. Because there was no alternative.

The heaviness pressed down even more. She shut her eyes, trying to bear it.

The doorbell was ringing. She heard it. Wanted it to stop. Ignored it. But it went on. Insistent. Intrusive.

She hauled herself to her feet and walked out into the hallway of the lofty high-ceilinged apartment. Her parents had a maid, but Fran had given her the day off, wanting only to be alone.

She reached to open the security locks of the double front door, then opened one side of it.

And slumped against the other side.

It was Nic.

He strode in, shutting the door behind him with a snap as she backed away. His eyes swept over her.

'Is it true?' he asked.

She stared, blinking at him. 'Is what true?' she said dimly. Faintness was drumming in her, a deluge of emotion swamping her.

His voice was terse. 'That you're pregnant.'

She stilled, turned to stone except for her eyes, which were dilating. 'How—?'

'Mantegna—he's just been to see me!' He bit out the words.

To tell me what I need to do—which he did not have to tell me. Which I knew from the very instant he said those words.

He could feel his guts twisting, feel so much more. A storm of emotion he could not deal with, like a tempest in his head. And then, slicing through him, came the sight of her swaying.

Fran felt the blood drain from her, dizziness pumping over her. She heard Nic give an oath, and then he'd closed the space between them, taken her arms, her weight against his shoulder.

He was guiding her through into her parents' opulent drawing room, with its gilded furniture, hand-blocked wallpaper, oil paintings on the walls. Was setting her down on a silk-upholstered eighteenth-century sofa. Standing in front her. Tall, overpowering. Demanding the truth.

The truth she had kept from him. Concealed. Because what would be the point in telling a man who did not want her that she carried his child? A child he would not want.

Through the stab of emotion she cursed Cesare for his interference.

Nic was speaking again, towering over her, demanding an answer.

'Tell me!' Something flashed across his face. 'I need to know!'

She took a breath like a razor in her lungs. A razor that cut through the emotions storming inside her—emotions that weren't relevant. That got in the way of what she must say.

She lifted her eyes to his, making herself

meet that demanding gaze. Steeling herself to speak.

'No, Nic, you don't need to know. And I didn't *want* you to know—what would be the point?'

She got to her feet. She would do this standing. Say what needed to be said. Keep all emotion out of it. For what use was emotion in such an impossible situation?

With a strength she called upon from a place she had not known she possessed, she spoke, making her voice clear.

'Nic, what happened in the States was a passing romance for both of us. We both knew that. And what happened in London was a mistake.' Her lips pressed together. 'We both know that too—you said as much to me, and I agree.'

She said the words calmly, as if calm was what she was feeling. She saw his face close.

'A mistake that has had consequences—' His voice was terse, clamping down on any other possibility.

She cut across him. 'Consequences that *I* shall cope with.' She lifted her chin, meeting his eyes head-on. Not flinching or floundering. Saying it straight out. 'Nic, I'll be living in America. You won't be troubled by me. I give you my word.'

With biting mockery she heard herself say what she had said to him that nightmare morning when he'd thrown her out of his bed, his life.

She took a breath, ploughing on. 'I'll be a single mother, and that will be fine. I'll probably work part time. I don't need a salary to live on. I have income enough of my own—a trust fund that was set up by my father when I was born. So you see—'

A hand slashed down through the air, silencing her.

'No. That will not be happening.' Nic's eyes were like sapphires, blue and hard. 'What will happen is that we shall marry.'

Fran stared, stopped in her tracks. 'You can't be serious...' The words fell from her, hollow and disbelieving.

'And *you* cannot think that I would say otherwise!' He shifted his stance, taking a breath. Emotion was churning in him—emotion he could make no sense of.

She was still staring at him as if he were

mad. As if he'd said the last thing she had expected him to say.

With an effort, she spoke. 'Nic, you made it clear you wanted nothing more to do with me. And now you speak of *marriage*?'

'Of course I do! Did you think I *wouldn't*?'

She shook her head. Dazed and confused and so much more. Abruptly, her legs weak, she sat down.

Nic went on standing, looking down at her. 'We'll marry and that is all there is to it. We'll have to sort out where we'll be living—if necessary I can move my base to the West Coast, if you intend to keep working, but if not then Rome would be best for me, if that suits you. We'll need to buy somewhere—a house or apartment suitable for us both, of course—but that won't be a problem, so—'

She held up a hand, consternation in her face. 'Nic, stop! *Stop!* You're making assumptions, taking it for granted that I— That we—'

His face hardened. 'Nothing else is possible,' he said tightly.

Emotion seared in him. *Because no child of mine will be born a bastard, as I was, even if it means I have to marry a woman I would never want to. A woman who represents everything I detest.*

He could hear the words in his head, hear himself incise them into his brain.

She was speaking again, and he made himself listen through the emotions searing through him.

'Nic, give me *time.*'

He slashed a hand through the air. 'We don't *have* time. You need to accept that we must marry as soon as possible.' His eyes flashed darkly. 'Make whatever arrangements you require.'

Whatever those were, he did not want anything other than a quick, private wedding, to get them legally married. His face set. At some point he would have to meet the precious Marchese and his Marchesa—her parents. His expression hardened. Not to mention all her aristocratic English relatives as well—like that gilded *ragazzo*…the young lordling knocking back champagne at Viscari's damned party. How many more of them were there? Dozens, probably. All those aristos were related to each other, so Italy would be crawling with them as well.

Her voice cut off his vicious thoughts. She was standing up again. Facing him off.

'Nic, listen to me. *Listen.*'

Fran's voice was like a knife, cutting through him.

'I am not going to marry you. There is no *need* for it.'

He stared at her. 'There is *every* need,' he ground out.

For one long, endless moment they stared at each other, the tension between them palpable. Then, out of nowhere, he felt his emotions change.

She carries my child. It grows within her. Invisible—but there. Binding me to her. And her to me. Beyond all that separates us.

He felt another wave of that emotion he could not explain except by thinking of the child, *his* child, growing within her, silently and invisibly.

He took her shoulders suddenly and felt her flinch, as if she had not expected it. Through the fine wool of her sweater she was warm beneath his touch. He caught the scent she was wearing and it lingered in his senses. Everything about her had *always* lingered in his senses.

His eyes held hers, lifted to his with confusion in them…uncertainty. Well, he would be certain for both of them.

'Fran…' It was the first time he'd said her name since their time together, all those long months ago—months during which he'd wanted to put her behind him, into the past where she needed to be.

But she wasn't in the past any longer. Because of his own madness that night when she'd come to him, his madness and his weakness, she was in his present and in his future.

He said her name again. Without the honorific. The honorific he did not want her to have. Then took a breath, his hands still closed over her shoulders.

'We can make this work. We can and we must.' He said what had to be said, in spite of what she had indicated with everything she had done since she had discovered she was pregnant with his child: the decision she had made to keep it from him, making assumptions about him that were not hers to make.

And now she was indicating with every proviso she put to him how little she wanted what she was going to have to do. What they were *both* going to have to do.

'I know it won't be easy, or straightforward. But it must be done.'

She looked at him sadly. Something seemed to have gone out of her, and there was defeat in her eyes now. 'Neither of us want this, do we?'

He didn't answer, and he didn't have to. She knew his answer. Knew it from his veiled eyes, from the sudden pressure of his hands over her shoulders. Those strong hands that had once caressed her body to ecstasy…

She tore her mind away. This was not the time or the place to think of that. She felt her heart start to hammer and stepped aside from him, making his hands fall away. She felt unsteady on her feet without them, but she ignored it.

'I think you should go now, Nic,' she said tiredly. 'We both need time to…to come to terms with this.'

He did not move. 'But you accept that we have no option but to marry?'

She heard that word again, floating in the

gaping space between them—unreal, so unreal, impossible to contemplate, whatever he said.

But face it she must.

He saw her tense her jaw, swallow. 'I—I suppose so.'

Defeat was still in her voice. It cut at him— just as it had when she had walked out of the elevator, as if turned to marble, after he had ordered her to leave him alone.

And now he was back at her side, and neither of them had a choice about it. Both had to accept what neither of them wanted to. Because there was nothing else to be done *but* accept it.

She ran a hand wearily over her forehead. 'I don't know what to think…what to do.'

'For now, nothing. Rest. We'll talk more this evening…make plans.' His voice was brisk, businesslike.

Her expression changed. 'Nic, not tonight. I can't. I'm meeting Cesare and his wife for dinner. It's all arranged.'

The blue eyes flashed. The word *Cancel!* hovered on Nic's lips, but then his expression changed.

'Then I'll come too,' he announced.

There was an edge in his voice. That damned

Cesare could put up with his company. And it would declare to Il Conte—and the world—that he and Fran were a couple now. Whatever her aristocratic friends and relations thought about her marrying a jumped-up *nouveau riche* billionaire, bred in the backstreets of Rome.

Fran was staring at him, her thoughts jangled. Maybe Nic *should* come tonight—maybe they needed to behave like an engaged couple, if that was what they were, what they would have to be now. And who better to start with than Carla and Cesare? Her mouth twisted. After all, it had been Cesare who'd sent Nic here, so he must have wanted this outcome to his interference.

And is this what I want? Nic forcing himself to marry me? Me forcing myself to marry him? Is this really what I want?

She felt emotion churn within her with a sickening sensation. Felt herself steel herself in response. Maybe it didn't matter what she felt about it—maybe Nic was right—maybe marrying each other was the only thing to be done…

'So, what time do you want me to collect you tonight?'

She focussed her thoughts away from the

enormity of even contemplating marrying the man in front of her—the man who had thrown her out of his bed, told her he wanted nothing more to do with her, and yet was now telling her they should marry.

'Um…about eight, if that's convenient? I'm meeting them at eight-thirty, and the traffic is always fiendish.' A thought suddenly struck her. 'Nic, it's at the Viscari. Carla always patronises it. But surely you won't want—?'

He gave a grim smile. 'I'll cope,' he said tightly. He slipped his hand inside his jacket pocket, drew out a card. 'This has my mobile number on it. Or my PA will put you through wherever I am.'

She took the card with nerveless fingers. 'I'd better give you mine as well,' she said.

We don't even know each other's phone numbers but we're going to marry each other.

A bead of hysteria at the enormity of what she was agreeing to formed in her throat. But then he was handing her another card to write on, and a pen to use. She recognised the make—custom-designed and exorbitantly expensive. Like nothing that Nic Rossi, who worked in security at a hotel in Nevada, could ever have aspired to.

She felt something rip inside her—a memory being torn up, its ragged shreds to be whipped away by the desert wind, lost for ever...

Handing back his pen with the card she'd written her phone number on, and taking his in exchange, she made herself look at him.

He isn't Nic Rossi. He never was. He's Nicolo Falcone, a billionaire who's forcing himself to marry a woman he doesn't want to marry just because she mistakenly got pregnant by him.

She felt her throat tighten and forced it open. What good was it to think of that? To remember the man she'd thought he was...the man he'd never been?

'Until tonight, then,' she said.

Donna Francesca speaking to Nicolo Falcone.

He took a visible breath as he stashed his pen, and the card she'd written on.

'Until tonight,' he said.

Then he strode from the room, from the apartment, and was gone.

Leaving behind the woman he was going to marry for the sake of the child she was carrying. For no other reason.

The words seared across his brain, etching their truth into his consciousness.

CHAPTER EIGHT

'THE VISCARI.' NIC'S instruction as the car pulled away from the kerb outside the Marchese d'Arromento's Rome apartment was curt.

His driver glanced round at him, as if questioning the instruction.

'You heard me,' Nic said, his tone grim.

He hadn't set foot in the Viscari Roma since walking out all those years ago, refusing to kowtow to the pampered stripling who'd been handed on a gilded plate the managerial post Nic had worked so hard to merit.

Beside him sat the reason he was now going to walk back in.

She'd slid into the back seat, murmuring a stilted, low-voiced greeting, but since then had said nothing. As the car moved into the infamous Rome traffic Nic looked across at her, taking in the chic but understated cocktail frock—a couture number, he saw at a glance—the elegant coil of her chignon at the nape of her neck, a double row of antique pearls looped over her bodice, matching pearl drops at her ears. Every inch La Donna Francesca.

Memory pierced him of how he'd critiqued the dress she'd been wearing that first evening he'd set eyes on her as suitable for an academic dinner, but not doing full justice to her breathtaking beauty.

Well, the dress she wore now certainly did do her justice, but he would have given a fortune to have her back as the woman she'd been then.

But she never was that woman. She was always La Donna Francesca, whatever she told you.

He cleared his mind. No point thinking about that...no point remembering what had been, or never been. No point doing anything but addressing the situation they both faced now: Nicolo Falcone marrying Donna Francesca di Ristori.

'Have you thought any more about our wedding?' he said abruptly.

Fran's eyes flickered to him. 'Not really,' she said.

It had been impossible to think about anything coherently. She'd spent the day in a kind of daze, still trying to come to terms with what she had agreed to do. It still seemed impossible, unreal—as unreal as going to dine at the Viscari with Nicolo Falcone.

She'd texted Carla to tell her that Nic would be with her that evening. She had added nothing more. Presumably Cesare would have informed his wife of his high-handed interference in her life. Now they could cope with the results. Starting with having dinner with both herself and the man she had, so it seemed, agreed to marry.

Her dazed thoughts whirled confusedly in her head. Finding no rest.

'Obviously you have the pick of any of my hotels,' Nic was saying now. 'Unless you want to be married from your home?'

He realised he had no idea where that was. Some *palazzo* or *castello* somewhere—but where? He would have to look it up. There would be plenty of information on her family if he consulted the genealogies of the Italian nobility. It was a world he didn't know and wasn't interested in. Had no sympathy with.

'No.' She shook her head. 'My sister's getting married there next year—a huge affair. I think one of your hotels sounds better. Maybe abroad?'

She shouldn't have said 'abroad'. Instantly in her mind's eye was the Falcone Nevada, an oasis of luxury, lapped by the desert, where she had taken Nic to be one of his own employees, taken off with him for the road trip that would change her life for ever. That had brought her to this destination now.

The tearing feeling assailed her again.

'What about the Caribbean?' Nic was continuing. 'I've got a good few there you can choose from.'

'I'm sure any one of them will be fine,' she answered.

She didn't mean to sound dismissive. It was just that the very thought of standing beside Nic, becoming his wife, seemed beyond unreal.

'I'll...um... I'll look them up on the internet,' she went on, trying to sound less blitzed.

The car was gliding up to the imposing frontage of the Viscari Roma. Nic climbed out, opening the passenger door for Fran, who got out gracefully.

Nic's eyes went to her. He felt his stomach clench, as it always did whenever he looked at her. *Per Dio*, how beautiful she was.

He crushed the reaction down. He was not marrying her for her beauty, but for the baby she carried.

The doorman was coming forward, his eyes registering exactly who it was walking into his employer's flagship hotel. A caustic smile tightened Nic's mouth. Fran seemed unaware, turning towards him.

'We're meeting Cesare and Carla in the cocktail lounge,' she said.

Nic's eyes were sweeping around the lobby, going to the service door behind Reception that led down to the basement where he had first worked—the lowest of the low, the humblest employee of all. As he went forward towards the cocktail lounge, which opened off the lobby, his face was set.

It stayed set as they approached the Conte and his Contessa. The former got to his feet, greeting Fran with a kiss on her cheek, and then turned to Nic.

'Falcone,' he said, and held out a hand to him.

For a moment Nic was motionless. Then, wordlessly, he took the outstretched hand. After all, had the illustrious Conte not wanted him to be here with his ex-fiancée he would not have deigned to inform Nic that there was any requirement to call upon Fran that morning.

'Signor Il Conte,' he acknowledged.

The handshake was brief. Cesare's hand was slim, but strong for all that, in Nic's larger hand. Then the Conte was introducing his wife, whom Fran was already greeting cordially.

'Contessa,' offered Nic dutifully.

He could see the Contessa's eyes were alive with curiosity. A dramatic brunette, her looks were a striking foil to Fran's pale blondeness, and her dress in dark cerise was a vivid contrast to Fran's eau de Nil. He wondered in passing whether he had ever seen her here at the hotel when he'd worked here, for she was, after all, Vito Viscari's late uncle's stepdaughter.

Nic and Fran took their seats and the Conte resumed his. For a moment there was silence, as if the full impact of just why he was there with his host's former fiancée was pressing upon them all. Then a waiter was there, the Viscari emblem blazoned on his shirt.

'Campari and soda, please,' Nic heard Fran say.

And as he heard it memory thrust into his head. It was the very drink she'd ordered that night he'd homed in on her. Was she remembering it too? He thought she was, for she suddenly paled.

He ordered a martini for himself and then sat back, crossing one leg confidently over the other. He was here in the Viscari Roma—enemy territory—and he was socialising with Il Conte di Mantegna, who had once thought to marry the woman that he, Nic, was in fact going to marry.

And no way—no way on God's earth—was Nicolo Falcone, who had dragged himself from slum kid to billionaire by his own efforts and had had *nothing* handed to him on a plate, going to do anything but own the evening.

'Francesca and I are trying to decide where to have our wedding,' he said, addressing his hosts, taking control of the conversation from the off, wanting nothing unspoken about why he was there. 'At the moment the Caribbean is the front runner. I have several properties there to choose from.'

'That sounds very romantic,' the Contessa said brightly, sipping at her drink.

It wasn't the best word to choose, and it hung awkwardly in the air.

Fran stepped into the gap. All the long-learned habits of social correctness slipping into gear. 'I don't really know the Caribbean,' she mused. 'How different are the islands?'

It started, as she'd hoped, a conversation—very civil, very anodyne, and completely masking the inherent strain of the situation—about the variety of islands to be found in the Caribbean. All seemed perfectly fine places to get married. Perfectly lovely. Perfectly acceptable. Perfectly—

Fran ran out of words to describe the place where she and Nic were likely to join their lives together. Unexpectedly. The word was utterly inadequate to describe the situation, as the prospect had only become real that morning.

Emotion jolted through her, but she pushed it aside. Not the time, not the place.

However, the subject of the Caribbean served its purpose and got them to the point of having menus discreetly handed to them. A discussion about food then followed, which got them through some more of the evening and was in turn followed by a discussion about which wines to choose.

A sommelier glided up to help them select the best from the extensive cellars the Viscari Roma had to offer its guests.

Nic glanced at the sommelier and recognised him. He raised a brief hand in casual greeting. 'Pietro—*ciao*.'

The other man's eyes flickered slightly, but all he said was, 'Good evening, Signor Falcone.'

Nic knew why, and acknowledged his professionalism. But there was no way he was going to blank this man he'd worked with when both of them had been juniors. Pietro in the kitchens and Nic as general dogsbody, his strong physique making him ideal for shifting furniture, unloading delivery lorries, and doing any other heavy lifting that was required.

He smiled. 'How are Maria and the children?'

Pietro had married his sweetheart—one of the chambermaids—and babies had swiftly followed.

Pietro nodded, but only as any member of staff might do to a guest. 'They are all very well, Signor Falcone.'

Nic's smile widened. 'I'm glad to hear it.'

He could see that Fran was looking at him, her gaze questioning. The Conte was looking as if the conversation were not taking place. His Contessa was observing with a look of lively curiosity on her face.

'Remember,' Nic went on addressing his erstwhile fellow staffer, 'if you ever want a change of scene from Viscari let me know—'

Tactfully, Pietro said nothing.

Nic's gaze swept back to his hosts. 'Pietro and I go back a long way. We both started work here at the same time, as teenagers,' he said.

The questioning look on Fran's face deepened. She was about to speak, but a voice behind Nic pre-empted her.

'Here to poach my staff now, Falcone, as well as my garden designer?'

Nic turned, not rushing the movement. He'd half expected this approach. His eyes glinted sapphire. 'Only if they want to improve their prospects—as I did,' he returned with pointed acerbity.

Vito Viscari did not deign to reply to that. Instead he simply went on, his cultured voice cool, his eyes watchful. 'And *is* headhunting the purpose of your patronage tonight?' he probed.

His body's stance radiated whatever the opposite of welcome was. Nic was only too aware of that. But before he could reply, he heard the Contessa interject.

'Vito, I left a message for you. Obviously you never picked it up.' She spoke casually, but there was a determined brightness to her voice. 'Signor Falcone is here with Francesca.'

Vito's cool gaze was suddenly sharp. 'Is he?'

'Yes,' corroborated Fran, knowing it was time to defuse the situation. She lifted her chin. 'I do hope that won't cause any problems, Vito?' Her question was as pointed as Nic's comment had been.

Vito smiled—a tight smile, but a smile nevertheless. It was a professional smile, Nic could tell instantly—one to use with an influential and favoured guest as, of course, was Donna Francesca di Ristori.

His own hackles were rising, just as they

always did when he encountered Vito Viscari. The only time they had not done so had
been during those heady days a year ago when,
armed with half the Viscari shares in his back
pocket, he'd been able to stride into Viscari
board meetings, and throw down a list of prime
properties he intended to move to the Falcone
brand.

A familiar stab of anger flared in him.
Thanks to Vito's mother-in-law his triumph
had turned to ashes. Nepotism had struck
again, balking him of his due.

'Not at all,' Vito was saying now, in reply to
Fran.

As if belatedly aware that one of his somme-
liers was waiting to discuss their wine for the
evening, he nodded across at Pietro.

'I'm interrupting—my apologies,' he said.
His eyes went back to his guests. 'Enjoy your
evening,' he said, his smile warmer now as it
encompassed the three people whose presence
in his hotel he did *not* begrudge.

He walked away and Nic heard the Conte
putting a question about a certain wine to
Pietro, who immediately got involved. Nic left

him to his discussion, aware that Fran wanted to speak to him.

'I didn't know you once worked *here*,' she said.

That air of puzzled questioning was still in her tone of voice, her eyes, and Nic knew she was remembering that conversation they'd had in the motel by the desert lake, and him telling her how he'd got his start in life. He felt more memories push at him, seeking entrance— memories of everything else that had happened at that humble lakeside motel.

He crushed them from him. Returned to the moment in hand. Pietro had left them, to find the wines selected for their evening.

'Yes, my first job was here, at sixteen. Right after the police made it clear it was either get work or be charged for assault for beating up the man beating up my mother.'

He was addressing the Conte and his Contessa now, not caring if he shocked them.

It didn't shock Fran, hearing me tell her that.

The thought was in his head even as he saw Il Conte's features tighten and the Contessa looking taken aback.

Then she rallied. 'So you came to work here?

I'm glad,' she said. 'My stepfather, Guido Viscari, was always keen on giving disadvantaged youngsters a start in life.'

'Oh, yes,' said Nic dryly, 'he certainly was happy to give us a *start*—providing we knew our place and kept to it.' *Like never aspiring to race up the management ladder ahead of his precious nephew.*

'Evidently he did not succeed in your case,' Cesare murmured dryly.

Nic's eyes flashed to his. 'Evidently not,' he agreed, with a tightness that was acerbic.

Then the maître d' was coming up to them, murmuring to Il Conte that their table was ready for them. Dutifully, they all got to their feet.

Fran, Nic could see, had an introspective air about her. He held out his arm. 'Shall we?' he said.

With a little start she rested her hand on his arm, and they followed behind the Conte and Contessa into the opulent dining room beyond the bar. It was the lightest of touches but he still caught her scent, a delicate, expensive fragrance, and felt it pluck at him.

He almost turned to look down at her and

smile, but then his attention was caught by another diner, whom he recognised as a society journalist who ran a diary column in one of the upmarket dailies. The Contessa had clearly spotted him too, and Nic recalled that she was some kind of journalist as well.

He watched as the Contessa murmured something *sotto voce* to her husband, resulting in a brief nod from him.

'It was inevitable.'

He caught Il Conte's reply, and knew what he was referring to.

He bent his head slightly towards Fran. 'It seems we may make a news item tomorrow morning,' he warned her.

Fran gave a little start again, and the Contessa explained. 'He won't be waspish. I know his style. But he will,' she went on, 'definitely speculate.'

'He may also feed the news to his colleague on the finance pages, given that it is Nicolo Falcone dining at the Viscari,' Cesare contributed.

Fran shut her eyes for a moment. She did not relish reading about herself and Nic in the morning papers.

I should have foreseen this.

Rome was such a hive of gossip, with everyone buzzing about what everyone else was doing, and who they were doing it with. Since living in the USA she'd forgotten just what a fishbowl it was. Belatedly, it dawned on her that the other diners here might well see her too, and speculate as to why she was here with Nicolo Falcone. And that might reach her parents.

I don't want them to find out like that. I have to tell them myself.

She gave a sigh, opening her eyes again. Letting her gaze go to Nic.

But he isn't Nic, is he? He's Nicolo Falcone, a man rich and powerful enough to provoke the interest of journalists.

'He's welcome to do so,' she heard him say, and there was a coldness in his voice that belonged to the billionaire hotelier, not to the man she had once known.

The arrival of their first course was a welcome diversion, and conversation returned to innocuous topics. Fran was grateful. Cesare, she could see, was exerting himself, though there was inevitably an air about him of what could only be deemed unconscious hauteur.

Beside him, Carla was being her usual incisive and forthright self.

But it wasn't her hosts who drew her attention. It was the man at her side.

Nic.

No, not Nic—Nicolo Falcone.

Her eyes flickered to him. That same overpowering impression she'd got of him in that disastrous exchange in the elevator at the Viscari St James's slammed into her. The laid-back, easy-going man she'd spent those glorious days with in America was gone. This was a man of formidable achievement, of huge wealth, of the power and self-assertion that went with that. A man who scarcely smiled...

Memory flashed through her of that slashing smile like a desert wolf, crinkling the vivid blue eyes, warming them on her...

She blinked and it vanished, and there was Nicolo Falcone once more, making some impatiently scathing comment about the latest government delays in respect of the topic they seemed to have moved on to—Italy's earthquake warning system. It was a subject Fran knew was of keen interest to Cesare, whose medieval *castello* was deep in the Apennine fastness, much prone to earthquakes.

'I considered opening a mountain resort there at some point, but it's just too risky,' Nic was saying.

'A pity—the area needs inward investment,' Cesare replied.

Nic's eyes flickered. Had that been intended as a criticism of him?

'Something that surely is the responsibility of the landowners?' he asserted.

Did aristocrats like Il Conte assume their effortlessly inherited wealth was there to spend on their own pleasures, not on the vast patrimony they possessed?

'Indeed,' acknowledged Cesare, and Fran could see his air of unconscious hauteur heightening. 'And I make considerable investment in the local economy of my estates,' he replied. 'My family has done so for centuries.'

He reached for his wine, the candlelight catching the gold of a signet ring incised with his family crest—a crouching lion, ready to attack. Nic felt his hackles bristle in response, just as they had when Vito had strolled over to challenge his presence on his territory.

It was Vito's step-cousin who spoke now. 'I hope you will visit Castello Mantegna one day with Francesca,' Carla said brightly. 'It's absolutely magnificent! For me, of course, the particular appeal is the artworks.'

She launched into a catalogue of her husband's collection and Fran joined in, making some remark about how she had enjoyed seeing them when she had last been there.

Then she halted. The last time she'd been to Cesare's *castello* had been when she had just become his fiancée. She had visited with her parents and siblings to celebrate their forthcoming union.

And now it's a completely different man I'm going to marry. Going to have *to marry.*

She felt emotions pulling inside her, tugging in different directions like ropes knotted inside her. Unconsciously she ran a hand over her abdomen. Unbelievable to think that silently, invisibly, a child was growing there—a child that would be both hers and the man's beside her... Uniting them.

Can anything unite us, though?

The question was unanswerable, impossible, and it hung silent in the space between them.

'Are you all right?' Nic's voice was suddenly low in her ear.

There was concern in his voice. But it was not for her, she knew. It was for the baby she carried—his son or daughter.

Impulsively she seized at the opportunity he'd presented with his enquiry. 'I do feel tired,' she admitted. 'It's been a long day...'

She let the sentence trail. 'Long' had not been the problem. Weariness washed over her.

'Perhaps I could just have coffee and skip dessert,' she said.

It was what they all did, and Fran was grateful. Grateful too for the desultory conversation that limped on, with Carla doing her best to be bright and Cesare still exerting himself. And Nic... She gave an inward sigh. Nic was still broadcasting on all frequencies that he was no longer the man she'd known.

At last the evening came to an end. It had been an ordeal—she could only call it that. Weariness assailed her, but it was a weariness of the spirit.

As she climbed into Nic's car she gave a sigh.

'What is it?' Nic's voice was taut as he sank heavily down beside her. His mood was grim.

Fran looked at him. 'I'm just not used to you being—well, who you really are.'

'Do you imagine it isn't the same for me?' he answered, and she could hear the edge in his voice that she had heard there for most of the evening.

She did not reply—what could she say?

'So, having got through an evening with the illustrious Conte di Mantegna and his Contessa,' Nic was saying now, that edge still in his voice, 'at what point will you be presenting me to your parents?'

Her expression flickered in the streetlights as the car made its way back to her parents' apartment.

'I'll need to tell them first,' she said. 'And I must make sure they don't hear it from any wretched gossip columnist!' She gave another sigh. It was all so complicated. So difficult. So—

Impossible—that's what it is.

But it didn't matter that it was impossible. It had to be done.

She took a breath. 'I don't know when. Sometime this week I must head back to Cambridge.

But maybe I can go via Milan and stop off at home first. Or maybe—'

'I could drive you.' Nic cut across her. 'And you can tell them with me there. There's no point prevaricating. The sooner the better. It has to be done.'

She shut her eyes. Yes, it had to be done—it *all* had to be done. She had to tell her parents, arrange a wedding somewhere, anywhere—it didn't matter—and Nicolo Falcone had to become her husband and—

Her thoughts cut out. It was impossible to think any further ahead.

They reached her parents' apartment and Nic helped her out. To her relief, he merely saw her to the door.

'Come for lunch with me tomorrow,' he said. 'I'll send a car to collect you.'

She shook her head. 'I don't want to eat out, Nic. Tonight was bad enough.'

His face tightened as they stood on the pavement. 'We need to talk. There are arrangements to be made.'

'Then come here for lunch,' she said.

He nodded, and they agreed a time. Then he

was climbing back into his car, nodding at the chauffeur, and the car was heading off again.

Wearily, Fran went upstairs. This time last night she had thought she was to be a single mother, and now…

'Come through into the dining room. It's just cold meat, bread and salad—I hope you don't mind. I always give the maid time off when I'm here. I don't need her.'

Fran led the way from the wide entrance hall into a room Nic had not seen the previous day, but it was similar to the one that he had seen. The same antique furniture—inherited, of course, not purchased, as his was at his headquarters and at his hotels—oil paintings on the wall, an abundance of silverware and porcelain. All the accoutrements of an aristocrat's town apartment.

His mouth twisted unconsciously.

A simple meal was set out on a long mahogany table. White wine was chilling in a cooler, and there was fruit on the sideboard.

He took the place Fran indicated. She was not wearing couture clothes today, just a pair of elegantly cut trousers and a pale green shirt with a white stripe running through it. Her hair was caught back in a switch, and she wore no make-up. It was impossible to tell that she was pregnant.

For a moment—just a moment—Nic found himself wondering whether he should ask for confirmation of her pregnancy. He frowned.

Maybe it was a false alarm...maybe I don't have to go through with this after all.

'What is it?' Fran's voice was cool as she directed the question to him, sitting down opposite him at the table and reaching for a linen napkin.

Nic started. Had she read his mind? No, for she was continuing in the same cool, challenging voice.

'Do you disapprove of something?' She lifted her hand to indicate their surroundings.

Nic heard the challenge in her voice—a coolness that had never been there with him before.

Into his head came a moment from their very first encounter at the bar in the Falcone Nevada—the way she had challenged him to name three astrophysicists to corroborate his blatant hook-up line that she did not look like the stereotypical image of one.

There had been humour in that challenge. Amusement. Engagement with him.

There was none of that now. Now she was simply Donna Francesca, expressing her displeasure at any criticism of her father the Marchese's choice of décor.

He shook his head, his expression shuttered. 'It's very elegant,' he said.

'It's old-fashioned,' she admitted, 'but I like it. It hasn't changed much since my grandparents' time. Or even before theirs, I suspect,' she added, trying to make her voice lighter.

But it was an effort to do so. Yet again into her mind shafted memories of how she had once been able to chat effortlessly with Nic, yet now she was conscious of the awkward restraint between them, making all conversation stilted. Laborious.

She indicated the spread on the table. 'Help yourself,' she said.

Memory shafted in her yet again—they'd had picnics en route several times on their road trip, stocking up at small town supermarkets, pulling over at viewpoints, eating out of paper bags...

She crushed the memories back. Those carefree days were gone. Now there were grimmer things to sort out.

'I think you're right about the Caribbean,' she said, watching him help himself to freshly bought rolls and multiple slices of ham and salami, remembering how hearty his appetite had always been, to feed that powerful frame of his.

She dragged her mind away from such memories, away from how his smooth-muscled torso had felt beneath her gliding fingertips.

'We should marry there, at one of your resorts.' She paused. 'But on our own.' She paused again, made herself look at him. 'It would be easier for my parents and...' she swallowed '...since you don't have any family—'

She broke off. That had been tactless. His glance at her was mordant, shuttered.

'Suits me,' he said, beginning to eat.

It was a laconic reply, but nothing like the laid-back way he'd spoken to her in America. This registered...*indifference*. A verbal shrug indicating how unimportant it was to him.

She blenched. Struggled on. Pushed a helping of salad around her plate. She wasn't hungry in the slightest. Just nauseous.

And not because of her pregnancy.

'It's going to be difficult for them, Nic. I can't help that. A shotgun wedding is never what parents want for their children.' She gave a heavy sigh. 'And an unintentional pregnancy is never ideal in the first place,' she finished.

Blue eyes lifted, skewered her. Anger was suddenly spearing through him.

'Did I *ask* you to come to me that night in London?'

The words stabbed from him and found their target. Fran blenched again as they impacted. He stabbed again.

'Don't blame *me* for your predicament. You're as responsible for this as I am. I made it clear to you that I did not want to continue our... *acquaintance*—' his mouth twisted on the word '—yet you persisted.'

His voice was icy—as icy as it had been in that elevator, telling her to make no further contact with him. She gave a cry, dropping her fork. Crested silver, he noticed absently.

'I'm *not* trying to blame you. I'm simply saying that no one should *have* to marry for the sake of a baby that wasn't planned.' She shut her eyes. Misery filled her suddenly.

Dear God, however were they to make this marriage he was insisting on work? It was impossible.

'Nic, it's *you* going on about getting married—not me!' Her eyes flew open again. 'I *told* you I was OK with being a single mother—'

'Well, I am *not* OK with that.'

His voice was grim and tight. He pushed his plate away. All appetite had left him. Hell, what a damnable mess this was. He stared across at the woman opposite him, his eyes hard. The woman he did not want to *have* to marry. The woman who came from a world he rejected and despised. The woman who so screamingly obviously considered it a massive problem for her, and for her precious aristocratic family, for her to be marrying *him*, a jumped-up slum kid.

His eyes targeted hers. She had paled, her face whitening, and for a moment—just a moment—it cut him to the quick. But then words were being spoken, and he could not call them back.

'You *will* marry me, Donna Francesca.' He deliberately used her title, incising each word so she could not mistake them. 'Because I will accept nothing else. I will hear no more about single motherhood.' His eyes were narrow shards of hardest sapphire. 'Tell your parents whatever you want—it's no concern of mine.'

He got to his feet, tossing aside his unused napkin—white damask, monogrammed.

'My only concern—my only *possible* concern—is for the baby you carry. Nothing else.'

He strode from the room, heart pounding. Emotion thundered in his ears. Deafening him to everything else in the universe.

Behind him Fran sat shaking, staring blindly at the abandoned meal. It had been a disaster.

Emotion wrenched in her, crushing and tearing.

This was never going to work.

CHAPTER NINE

Nic THREW HIMSELF back into the chair behind his desk in his office, his face still thunderous. But his anger was at himself now. How had he lost it like that? What help was that? To let rip as he had?

He swore, descriptively and crudely, and was glad no one could hear him.

Yet for all the anger targeted at himself for losing his rag like that, and the guilt that he had done so to a pregnant woman, he knew that his hackles were still up. And he could find no way to lower them.

He didn't want to marry her.

Correction, I don't want to marry the woman she is—Donna Francesca di Ristori! Who comes with a whole baggage train of relatives I want nothing to do with, who'll be appalled and dismayed at her marriage to me.

His face tautened. It was who she was that was the problem. The very person she was....

In his head, fleetingly, like smoke from a campfire, memory caught. Once she had not been that person. Once she had been someone quite, quite different.

He pushed it away. She had never been that person—*never*. She had only ever been the person she was. The person he deplored, wished with all his being she was not.

Grimly, he stared out into the emptiness of his office, at the papal splendour he'd acquired second-hand, with money. In his mind's eye he saw the Marchese's grand apartment, resplendent with historic inherited possessions, each one ramming home to him the difference between them—between the Marchese's daughter and the self-made billionaire from the back streets of Rome.

Privilege—the privilege of birth and an effortlessly inherited right of wealth and nobility and social prominence, taking it all for granted.

That was *her* world. Not his.

Roughly, he reached for his computer, flicking it on. What point was there in dwelling on what could not be changed? He had work to do.

His mouth twisted and he started to bury himself in the day's business.

How long he worked he was not aware. He was aware only that his PA was coughing nervously at his office doorway.

'Signor Falcone, there is a visitor.'

His head lifted from his focus on his screen, brows beetling. A sense of *déjà vu* hit him—how his PA had a mere forty-eight hours ago announced the illustrious Conte di Mantegna, who had come strolling in to blow his world apart.

'Who?' he demanded tersely.

'Dottore Ristori,' his PA said cautiously, reading his grim mood.

Nic stilled. OK, so she wanted to play it that way, did she? Pretend she wasn't who she was.

He sat back in his chair, curtly indicating that she be shown in.

Fran walked in, still in the same outfit she'd had on when he'd arrived at the Marchese's apartment. But her face was set and strained.

'I need to talk to you,' she said without preamble.

He'd risen to his feet automatically and now came around his desk, indicating the pair of gilded *fauteuils* that flanked a small ormolu table where he received his informal appointments. He became conscious that he was feeling as warily constrained as he had been when her ex-fiancé had walked in as if he owned the place.

His expression closed, guarded, he waited to hear what she had to say. Giving nothing away until she had spoken.

She sat herself down on one of the chairs, set her handbag on the delicate table. He took the other chair. For a moment, a measurable passage of time, she said nothing. But her face was still drawn.

Something moved in Nic, but he quelled it. He wanted to know what she had to say.

A moment later she had said it—and it silenced him.

'Why do you hate me so much now, Nic?'

The words fell into the space between them.

He stiffened, and frowned. Whatever he had been expecting, it had not been that.

'I don't hate you.' His voice was clipped and tight.

She shook her head, rejecting his denial. 'Nic, your hostility to me is radiating off you like a star going supernova. I might think it's just because I'm pregnant, and the news is as unwelcome to you as I always knew it was going to be. Which is why I'm cursing Cesare for interfering, telling you what I knew you would not want to know. But it's not just that, is it? It's been like that ever since Cesare and Vito did their *Begone, lowly peasant!* routine on you at that wretched roof party.'

She took a razored breath. It had taken all her nerve to come here and confront Nic like this, but she was making herself do it. If their marriage—*if* it ever happened!—was to have *any* chance at all, she had to confront him now, not let it fester.

I won't have that! I won't have him bristling at me, blaming me, resenting me.

'So tell me, Nic. Tell me to my face. Why are you so damn *angry* with me?' She took another shuddering breath, leaning forward now. 'That night you blame *me* for—I *wasn't* damn well throwing myself at you. All I wanted, Nic, was to make peace with you. Because, like I said to you at the time, we had parted friends. So I don't see why discovering that *both* of us have other identities has made everything so damn difficult between us. I want you to explain that, Nic, I really do.'

She fell back, breathless, lungs heaving.

He'd heard her out, but she could see in the tense, taut features of his face that a nerve was ticking at his cheekbone, indicating the self-control he was exerting. She didn't care—she was beyond caring. She'd forced herself here and now she wanted answers. Answers she hadn't got that night at his hotel. She wanted to give a hysterical laugh. The night that had resulted in her presence here now.

He looked at her. Looked with those blue, blue eyes that had once poured all his hot desire into hers, but now which were as chill as Arctic ice, as remote as the upper layers of the atmosphere before it dissipated into black frozen space.

'It's very simple,' he said. 'I don't like who you are.'

She stared at him. 'I don't understand...' she said faintly.

He gave a rasp in his throat. 'I don't like everything you stand for!' he spelt out. 'I don't like the world you come from. I don't like the world *any* of you come from. I don't like your precious ex-fiancé, the illustrious Conte di Mantegna, and I don't like the man his wife is related to—that pampered playboy Vito Viscari, who had *everything* handed to him on a plate without working for it, without effort, without anything other than being born to it. I don't like anything about that world and I want nothing to do with it. But I'm going to have to.' His voice hardened. 'Because I have to marry *you*.'

She was silent, hearing him out. Then, in a low, emotional voice she said, 'I can't help who I am, Nic, any more than you can.' Her gaze flickered. 'And if you want my reply, I can tell you something as well.' She took a breath. 'I don't like the man *you* are, Nicolo Falcone. I don't like him at all, and I don't want to marry him.'

She got up, her hand splayed over her abdomen in an instinctive protective gesture. She could feel her blood surging in her veins, feel adrenaline pushing it around, and there was a tightness in her lungs, a sickness in her very being.

She looked at him. He hadn't stood up when she had, and he seemed to be frozen in his seat. Her eyes rested on him. It was strange... He looked so like Nic, the man she had known long ago. Nic Rossi, with his easy laugh and his laid-back charm and the teasing humour in his smile. But he wasn't that man at all.

'We're strangers,' she said quietly. 'And strangers should never marry.' She took a breath. 'Goodbye, Nic.'

Her hand pressed on her body, where their baby, secret and silent, lived and grew. She would have to sort something out eventually, but not now.

'We'll share custody, Nic—somehow, when the time comes. But I can't cope with that right now. I can't cope with anything.'

She looked at him, and something like a shard of glass pierced her. She did not let herself feel it.

'I'm going now,' she said. 'Please don't try and stop me.'

He didn't. He let her go. Let her walk out of his office, his space, his life.

Taking their child with her.

And he could not move. Not a muscle.

CHAPTER TEN

FRAN CLIMBED INTO the hotel shuttle bus at San Francisco airport. It had been a long flight, and it had come after a gruelling few days. She had flown out of Rome the very afternoon after confronting Nic, not able to bear to stay longer, then landed at Stanstead, taken the bus to Cambridge.

She had spoken to her professor the next morning, telling him she had to leave as soon as possible for urgent personal reasons. Replied to the email sitting in her inbox, accepting an invitation to an interview for a research position at a university in Southern California that she'd applied for when she'd discovered she was pregnant by a man who did not want her.

Her throat tightened unbearably. Now it was *she* who did not want *him*. Not the man he was.

And now, it seemed, with bitter irony, it was *he* who wanted *her*—or rather the baby she carried.

He was still determined on them marrying. And to that end there had come a slew of emails from him, and text messages, and voicemails, and calls she had ignored just as she'd ignored all his other attempts to communicate with her.

Because she knew what he was saying. The first message from him had said it all.

You're emotional—I understand that. But we can't leave it like this. When you've calmed down we can talk. For now, I'll leave you in peace. Then I'll come and see you in Cambridge and we can sort things out. We have no choice but to sort things out.

She'd deleted the message. And all the others. Only as she'd sat in Departures at Heathrow had she texted him. One final text before boarding.

She had flown quite deliberately to San Francisco. She had somewhere to go before she headed for LA. Somewhere she *had* to go.

As she checked in to her hotel, hearing the familiar American accents all around her, hearing herself being called Dr Ristori in the way she was used to here, she felt a sense of familiarity, of ease.

It comforted her.

But it brought memories too. Memories that she could not keep out. Memories that came of their own volition. That brought their own pain with them. It was a pain she would have to bear now. Memories of a tall, powerfully built, sable-haired guy with blue, blue eyes and a smile like a desert wolf.

Who was lost to her for ever.

And there was only one place to bear that. The place where she was going now.

Nic stared at the words on the phone screen as if they made no sense. But then, they didn't. They didn't make sense at all.

Nic, I'm not going to marry you. It would be a disaster for both of us. Neither of us is who we once thought we were. You aren't the man I remember, and I am not the woman you remember. We are better off without each other. Please don't try and make me change my mind, because I won't. I can't. We have well over half a year to sort out things like access rights. I'm sure we can come to a civilised arrangement. For now, I can't cope with that.

He kept reading the words, re-reading them. But still they made no sense. How could they? The imperative of their marriage was paramount. Except... His eyes rested on the words on the screen. For her, that imperative was absent.

We are better off without each other.

He read the words, read them again. Something was building in him. Something he didn't know, didn't recognise. But it was powerful. As if pressure were building up inside a volcano—a volcano that had been consigned to dormancy. Mistakenly.

His eyes moved back to the sentence that came before.

You aren't the man I remember.

He felt the pressure mount within him. His phone was ringing—his PA—but he lifted it only to slam the receiver down again. His focus was on the words, only on the words. And on the sense of pressure building in him. On the words that came next.

I am not the woman you remember.

And the pressure inside his head burst, flowing through his consciousness like lava racing down a mountainside, consuming everything in its path. He was remembering the woman he had once thought her to be. Remembering in absolute coruscating detail every single moment of their time together.

And with that came a realisation, blasting through everything else.

His phone rang again, and this time he snatched it up. 'Charter a plane to Cambridge, England—*now!*'

Fran was deplaning again, this time in Las Vegas. To walk out of McCarran had been to feel her throat spasm, as if she could see herself there in the summer heat, backpack on one shoulder, that last hurried kiss with Nic...

The rental car she picked up was no luxury SUV. Thoughts flashed through her of how she'd been so concerned that Nic had blithely helped himself to a hotel vehicle to take off in—

and how that other security guy had greeted him on their return from the desert sunset.

'Evening, boss.'

'He's on my team,' Nic had explained casually.

Yes, you might say that—you might also say that your team ran to thousands of people all around the world.

And all the time he was Nicolo Falcone, and I never noticed...

Getting out of Vegas occupied her mind, and she was glad to hit Route 15, out of the city, heading north-east. She would need to break her journey, stop off overnight, but that should be no problem. The problem would come later—closer to her destination.

Winter was closing in, and though she'd checked the forecast, and it had been sufficiently clement, snow would stop her in her tracks.

She drove on, determined to make her destination. Expression set.

Nic was throwing his weight around. He knew it and didn't care. That was what it was for. He was shamelessly using a mixture of arrogant imperiousness and calculated charm to get the information he wanted. *Needed.*

His eyes flashed blue fire. *Where the hell was she?*

Because she wasn't in Cambridge. Her departmental secretary was looking at him apologetically. 'You've just missed her, I'm afraid. She's gone to California—for an interview I believe.'

He strode off, claws clenching inside him. Then his phone was in his hand, and he was straight through to his own security team at his Mayfair property.

'I need you to trace someone,' was his terse command.

It was a simple order, but it took a frustratingly long time for the answer to get back to him. And when it did it stopped him in his tracks. Then galvanised him with the very first emotion he'd felt since he'd opened her email, in which she had refused to marry him.

Something that he could clutch at.

Hope.

Fran heaved a sigh of relief. The snow had not come, the road was still open, and day tickets were still available. She drove on between the dark conifers, all signs of habitation long gone, and then finally she was there, leaving the car in the almost deserted car park, making her way to where she wanted to be.

To remember what had never happened. What now never could.

She sat on one of the many benches, huddled into the ski-jacket she'd bought en route, her feet warm in the solid boots she'd also bought. The cold nipped at her, and she glanced at some of the few hikers, even more warmly clad than her, ready to go backpacking even at this time of year.

The sky above was leaden, but that did not spoil the view.

Ten miles across. Ten miles to where she had stood in the summer heat. She sat and gazed across the unbridgeable distance from there to here, to where she was now. Here at this point in her life.

We can't go back. We can't get back to what has gone. That time has past.

Wasn't that what she'd told herself in all those months since then? She told it to herself again—because she must. Because there was no alternative. This journey here, now, had been for one reason only. To finally say goodbye to that time. To finally let it go.

To let Nic go—the man she had come to say goodbye to.

Silently her hand went to her abdomen and she spoke to her unborn child, who still seemed so unreal, but who was there, secret inside her. Her voice was low, but clear in the cold air, here where there was no one else but the hikers starting their descent. So she spoke aloud the words she needed to say. To the child she needed to say them to. About the man she needed to say them for.

'I've brought you here so I can tell you, in years to come, that I made it here. But only on my own—only with you. And I want you to know that on that far side of here, ten miles away, I once stood—but not with you. I want you to know, my son or my daughter, that it was the most important time of my life. But I didn't know it then.'

She had thought herself alone, unheard by anyone but the tiny being growing within her.

But she was wrong.

A voice behind her spoke.

'And no more did I know it.'

A gasp broke from her. Instant recognition of that deep, gravelled voice, charged with so much.

She slewed around. Felt faint suddenly with shock. With so much more than shock.

It was Nic.

CHAPTER ELEVEN

FRAN'S EYES LEAPT WIDE. She got to her feet, impelled upwards. 'How—?' The most banal of questions. The most irrelevant.

He walked towards her. Like her, he was enveloped in a ski-jacket, thick boots on his feet, crunching on the stony path.

'My security team found you,' he told her. 'They're good at their job.' He took a breath. 'I was always glad you assumed I was one of them.'

'You *let* me think that,' she countered.

Her mind was reeling, but it was impossible to say anything else. Nic—*Nic,* here? It made no *sense.*

'Just as you let me think things about you.'

She gave a sigh. 'It was what we both wanted at the time.'

'Ah, yes,' said Nic. His hands were plunged into the pockets of his jacket. 'At the time.'

He paused, his eyes resting on her. 'And now? Now what is it that we want?'

She let her gaze slip away, and there was sadness in her voice. 'Different things. Impossible to reconcile. You're forcing yourself to marry me, and I don't want that. I don't want to marry a man who hates everything about me. A man I don't like for that very reason.'

'Is that so?' A studied neutrality filled his words. As if he were balanced on the point of a sword so sharp it could slice away his life with the merest slip.

'Yes!' There was vehemence in her voice—there had to be. How could she be standing here, thousands of miles from Rome, and Nic be standing here too? Having this conversation. A conversation that was a waste of time, of effort.

A waste of so much.

Emotion burned in her throat. Made her words sound as if they were wrung from her. 'Oh, Nic, you shouldn't have come here. It serves no purpose. It changes nothing. You're still Nicolo Falcone and I'm still Donna Francesca. We're strangers to each other. Strangers who deplore what the other is—strangers who by mistake have created a child between them, but strangers still.'

He nodded. He was keeping himself under control, because it was essential to do so. Just as it had been on his journey here—on the flight to Salt Lake City, closer to here than San Francisco, gaining him time on her, and then on the pedal-to-the-metal drive south, guided only by what his security team had uncovered.

She'd never flown to LA. She'd flown via San Francisco instead, then taken another flight to Vegas. Picked up a hire car there. Asked the clerk about winter closures, revealing her destination. Giving him the chance to get here in time.

To say what he had to say.

On which so much hung.

More than I ever knew. Could ever know. Until she walked away from me.

'Yes,' he said now, his tone still measured, his hands plunged deep into his pockets, where she could not see them clench with the exertion of the emotion that it was so essential to keep from her.

For now—or else for ever.

'Yes, strangers. The aristocratic Donna Fran-

cesca and the *nouveau riche* Nicolo Falcone.'
He took a breath, felt the cold air rushing into
his lungs. 'But there are two people who *aren't*
strangers.'

He paused again. He had to get this right. He
had only one chance, and on it everything de-
pended. *Everything.*

'Two people,' he went on, his eyes never
leaving her, 'who met as strangers but parted
as lovers. Nic Rossi and Doc Fran.'

Doc Fran. The sound of his affectionate
name for her rang in her ears, clutched at something inside her. She wanted to cry out, but was
silent. Silent as she stood there, unable to move,
unable to do anything but hear his words, as
still he spoke to her.

His eyes were fixed on hers, willing her to
listen. To believe. Believe what he was telling
her, what he *must* tell her. His voice took on
an intensity that caught at her, made her take
a breath in.

'Fran, why—*why*—when we first met, do
you think we never told each other who we
were? Why did we want to be the person each
of us presented ourselves as being? Because,'
he spelt it out now, finally, urgent to make her

understand, 'we didn't want to be weighed down by the rest of who we are! We wanted to be free of that.' She must understand him, surely she must—

Her eyes were widening, wondering, taking in his words. Letting them make sense inside her.

Then she heard herself answer him.

'Here in the USA I've never had to be *Donna Francesca*,' she said. 'I could just be...myself.' She looked at him. 'The person I would have been but for an accident of birth. With no expectations on me to marry a man like Cesare, to be his Contessa, fulfilling my mother's dreams instead of my own.'

He nodded slowly, his eyes never leaving hers, filling with new self-knowledge. 'I liked it that you thought me just one of the security team. It meant I didn't have to be Nicolo Falcone, endlessly proving the world wrong about me. Proving I could outsoar Viscari.'

Her expression changed. She was reminiscing. 'I remember how you said it was defeatist to accept the universe as it is.'

His blue-eyed gaze drifted across her face. 'I remember the fire in your eyes as you talked to

me about the stars. The passion in your voice.'
His expression changed again—changed to one
that started to melt the bones in her body. 'And
not just a passion for the stars.'

She gave a smothered cry, backing away.
'But that's gone. You made it clear enough that
night I came to your hotel.'

His eyes flashed. 'I was telling Donna Francesca.' He took a shuddering breath, making
himself say what he knew now was the truth.
The truth he had tried to twist into knots inside him. 'I used it—used your being Donna
Francesca—to send you away.' He shook his
head slowly, as if clearing something from it.
'But that wasn't the reason. I was lying to myself—to you.'

His mouth set and his gaze turned inward.

'All my life,' he said slowly, finding the familiar thoughts that had controlled him all his
life hard to put into bare, bald words, 'I have
feared being as my father was—a man who left
my mother pregnant with me. It was why I was
so insistent that we marry. All my life I have
vowed I would not be like him. And the simplest, surest way to not be like that was never to
let any woman close to me. So I would always

part from women, thankful to do so, thankful they had not come to rely on me, to hope for what I dared not offer them. And that,' he said, 'is what I did with you—as I have with all the other women who have passed through my life.'

His face worked.

'Except you were never like any of those women. Right from the start you were different.' He paused. 'Special. Like no other woman I've known.'

He took another breath.

'So when I saw you again, that night in London—saw you again when I had thought never to do so—all I knew was an overwhelming rush of something I had never felt before, never allowed myself to feel. You made every other woman in the world disappear for me. And that showed me...' His voice changed, dropped. 'Showed me the danger I was in—'

He broke off.

'I had to find something—anything—to keep you at bay. So I used the revelation of who you were as a way of doing that.'

Fran's eyes shadowed. She had her own truth to face. One that she had hidden from herself.

'I told myself that night when I came to your hotel that I simply wanted to make my peace with you—that I couldn't bear your cold rejection just because I hadn't told you the truth about myself, because I'd seemed so friendly with Vito Viscari. But I was lying to myself. I know that now. I came to you for one reason only.'

Her voice changed, became charged with intensity.

'I came to you because the first emotion that leapt in me when I saw you again was *joy*, Nic. Overwhelming joy. And I wanted to find you again—the Nic I'd known here, in our time together. That's why I came to you that night… the true reason that I blinded myself to.'

Emotion filled her, full, and choking, so that she could hardly breathe. Could not look at him.

She walked away from him, moving to the low wall that separated the terrace from the rough ground beyond, where it started its precipitous plunge a mile deep into the earth. She gazed out across the gaping distance to the rim so far away. Where once they had stood together, hand in hand.

But now…?

The question hung in the air—hung in the great gap of space that yawned over the plunging canyon.

Nic spoke behind her quietly, his voice low. 'We never made it here, to the North Rim, did we?' he said. He paused, and in the silence stretched all that he had come here for. 'But we're here now.'

She did not answer—could not. He came to stand beside her and she felt the powerful sense of his presence at her side.

'We're here now,' he said again.

And still she could not answer.

He spoke again, in that quiet, deep voice.

'What are names? Nic Rossi or Nicolo Falcone. Doc Fran or Donna Francesca. What are names compared with who *we* are? And why…?' He drew a breath. 'Why should they imprison us? Why should *we* imprison ourselves? Why should I let my poor mother's fears be fulfilled in me? Why would I be as faithless as my father, abandon my own child as he did? If I think it's defeatist to stick with the universe as is, then it's even more defeatist for me to think I would be like my father.'

He took another breath, drawing cold air into his lungs.

'Because of that I let you go, telling myself it was the right thing to do. And I did not seek you out again.'

Fran spoke, finding the words to say. 'I thought to make contact again, but I couldn't find you—and you had made no contact with me. I had to accept it was over. That I had to move on. I told myself you had been the confirmation of my decision not to marry Cesare. Told myself that because letting go of Cesare had been easy it would be just as easy to let go of you, too—'

She broke off.

'It wasn't easy. *Isn't* easy.' She looked at him, her face strained. 'It wasn't easy to tell you I wouldn't marry you.'

She sensed his body, so close to her but not touching, tense.

'So why not ask yourself *why* it isn't easy?'

The question came from him. Not accusing. Only setting it between them. Needing an answer.

She could not give one. For tears were spilling, silently, and she could not stop them, could do nothing but stand there, full of so much she could not speak of.

Silence netted them. Silence and the chill wind blowing down from the north.

Nic spoke. His eyes fixed on the far horizon to the south.

'Your answer is the same answer I will give,' Nic said, in that quiet, deep voice. 'The answer that brought me here to join you, to where you, too, have come. For the same reason I have come here, giving the same answer to the same question. Come here to the destination we never made it to on our road trip together.'

There was a sudden unbearable tightening in his throat, and as if of its own volition, his hand reached for hers, meshing their fingers tightly.

'The destination we've reached now. Here…' He paused. 'Together.'

A sob choked from her, impossible to stifle, to deny, as impossible to stop as it was to stop her fingers clutching at his, crushing them with hers, desperate and clinging. Instantly his own grip tightened on her hand and he swept her bodily into him. Folding her to him as she wept against him, sobs racking from her, breaking free at last of all that had held them back, bringing to her a release that flooded through her.

He let her weep, cradling her against him, his strength supporting her in her storm of tears.

His arms tightened about her as words broke from him. 'Don't leave me. I can't bear it if you leave me.'

The cry came from deep inside, from a place he'd never acknowledged could ever exist. But it blazed within him now.

She couldn't speak—not in words. But her hands clutched at his body, convulsing over the thick material of his jacket.

'Fran, *this* is us. This is who we are. We knew that, felt it when we were together, but we did nothing about it. We let life take us in different directions. But we should never have let that happen.'

He was guiding her forward, sitting her down on the bench she'd leapt from at his approach, lowering himself down beside her, his arm still around her shoulder. She buried her face in his chest, tears still streaming uncontrollably.

His mouth smoothed the golden tresses of her hair. 'Shall I say it first? Say what the truth is between us that we have been too blind to face?'

He lifted her face from his shoulder, let his blue, blue gaze pour into hers.

'You said we were good when we were together, but we were more than good. We were *right* for each other. Right as only two people who should spend the rest of their lives together are right for each other. *That's* what we had—that's what we recognised in each other but never said out loud. Well, now I *do*. I say it out loud—to you, here and now.'

He took a ragged breath, never letting go her gaze as she lifted it to his, yearning for his. He was filled with an emotion so strong it overpowered him, yet through it he spoke again. And each word bound him to her with bonds that would never break, *could* never break. Not now. Not ever.

'I know, Fran, with every fibre of my being, that you recognised that too and still do.' He paused, and she could hear the catch in his voice, felt her heart turn over at it. 'And you always will. For we have it again, and more, that rightness between us. The rightness of our love.'

He cupped her face with his hands, cradling it between his strong, tender fingers. His eyes pouring into hers.

'The love of Nic Rossi for Doc Fran—*and*, yes, the love between the people we also are, if we can accept it in each other. Nicolo Falcone and Donna Francesca. They too can love each other now.'

His voice changed, became edged with the bitterness engendered in him long, long ago.

'I know I will hardly be welcomed by your family—a self-made, fatherless slum kid—'

Her fingers flew to his mouth to silence him. Emotion was streaming through her as strong as the dazzling radiance of the universe, joy and wonder and a rapture she had never known till now. But she had to speak. To counter what he'd just said. Set it to rest for ever.

'How can you *say* that? You're a billionaire hotelier! You could probably buy and sell my father ten times over.'

Her voice changed, became strained, and her eyes searched his painfully as she lifted his hands away, folding them within her own, impressing upon them the fearful emotion she felt suddenly.

'I don't want you despising me for an accident of birth. I can't help being who I was born, any more than you can.'

'I know that,' he acknowledged heavily. His expression became shadowed. 'But I've had to fight for everything I ever had, and I've always despised those who have it handed to them on a plate, despised everything they stand for. All that the likes of Vito Viscari stand for. I have done right from the moment he appeared, fresh out of university and wet behind the ears, and his uncle gave him the managerial position I had worked my guts out to deserve in years of hard, unrelenting slog. Right to the moment his wife's mother gave him back the shares I'd seized from him in my takeover bid.'

She rested her forehead against the strong wall of his chest, his hands still folded within hers, feeling his heart pounding within. Then, abruptly, she lifted her head away.

'Nic.' Her voice was urgent. 'You *have* to let go of such feelings.' She guided his right hand, deliberately sliding it beneath the thick quilting of her jacket, across the soft warmth of her body beneath. She felt him start, but ignored it. She pressed her own hand over his, keeping it there.

'Our baby, Nic,' she said. 'Our baby will be born to *both* our heritages. Its grandfather will be a *marchese*, its great-grandfather a duke, and it will be heir to *your* billions. Are you going to despise *it* for the circumstances of its birth?'

She nodded slowly as she went on, his silence giving her the answer she knew he must give.

'You see?' she said softly.

She slid her fingers into his, rounded on her still slender frame within which their baby nestled, safe and protected. Growing to become the child they had created between them.

Our baby is real. Growing and living.

Wonder filled her, and a feeling of thankfulness that was an embrace to the baby deep within her.

A baby...a mother...a father. A family.

Emotion caught at her throat and she leaned into the strong body of the man with whom she had created such a miracle. A sense of peace possessed her now, after the tumult of her tears. A peace so profound and a sense of wonder so radiant in her mind, her heart, that she could scarcely bear it.

She had come here, to the destination they had never reached on that road trip that had ended before it should, to say goodbye to him. But now—ah, now—

Joy flamed in her—the same sudden blaze that had filled her when she'd seen him after all those months in London, but more...oh, so much more!

Could they really, truly be here together? United like this?

His hand was on her belly, and her hand was on his, and beneath them both the baby they had made was growing silently and secretly. For the first time she gave a little gasp of wonder. For the first time it was real to her. And as she cradled the tiny being, and he did too, for the first time she felt the wondrous reality of conception like a flower opening within her.

We've made it real. Made it real because now we are real together too! Nic and Fran... Nicolo and Francesca. And we are all the family we shall make together, when our baby is born to us.

Love poured through her—love for her baby,

love for the man she had created it with. Love that she had never known nor had thought to feel. But now it was alight in her—a flame that could never be quenched.

She lifted her face to his, all that she felt blazing in her gaze, clinging to him, their arms around each other.

'Am I dreaming this?' There was a smile in her eyes, a yearning.

His sapphire eyes burned down to hers. And in them she could see, with glory in her heart, that same emotion she felt for him. Pouring from him.

'Whatever name you call me by I am here for you. My own, my beloved, my most beautiful and exquisite Donna Francesca and my incandescent Doc Fran, who sets the heavens ablaze with her passion for them and sets me ablaze too.'

She caught his face with her hands, cupping his strong jaw, her thumbs on the mouth that could smile like a desert wolf but could also kiss with the velvet touch that had melted her from the first time he had ever taken her into his strong arms.

Her eyes poured into his. 'I told you I didn't

like you, Nicolo Falcone, but that isn't true. For you are still Nic, and you always will be. Nic Rossi—the man I fell for, the man I went *Wow!* over the first time he came across to chat me up. And if I admired and respected you then...' there was a little choke in her voice '...knowing you'd made good out of the rubbish childhood you had—well, how much more do I admire and respect you for the dizzying heights you've climbed as Nicolo Falcone? You've fought such battles and won them all.'

An acerbic glint showed in his blue, blue eyes. 'I lost my takeover of Viscari,' he corrected her.

She waved it away with her hand. 'And I'm glad you did. You don't have to prove anything to him any more. Or to anyone. Let Vito have his hotels and you have yours.'

She paused for a moment, wanting to say what it was important for him to hear.

'Nic, I know from my own field that all each of us needs is the zeal to excel. I don't have to prove I'm better than any other researcher. I just have to find out that bit more about the universe than anyone knows at the time when I publish my latest paper. I don't have to resent any other researcher for doing the same with their new bit of knowledge.'

Her voice changed.

'You have nothing more to prove to Vito! Nothing more to resent in him. You've got your fabulous empire, made all by yourself, through your own efforts and talents—now just *enjoy* it.' She smiled at him. A warm, true smile. 'Let's just enjoy it *all*, Nic—everything that life has blessed us with. I've won my own battles too. I've got my research career, and it's all I ever wanted to achieve. But now—'

She broke off. Took his hand, placed it once more where their child was growing silently, invisibly.

'Now I have even more. *We* have so much more! We have each other and we have our baby.' She gave a little choke, realising another truth. 'The baby brought us back together, Nic, and that is worth more than any number of research papers, any number of luxury hotels!'

His eyes held hers, so blue, so long-lashed, so absolutely precious to her.

'My wise, wise beloved,' he said.

His hand splayed across her slow-ripening body, splayed upwards to touch the soft swell of her breasts. She felt her heart begin to quicken as his expression changed, the glint in his eyes now blissfully familiar. As blissfully familiar as it was in her own.

He said her name—a low growl now—and she lifted her face to his, her heart full, lips parting in a sigh of expectation, of fulfilment to come.

His kiss was like slow velvet, playing on her lips, opening her mouth to him, soft and sweet and sensual. She felt her pulse quicken more, and warmth spread in her body as her hand slid under his jacket to feel the muscled strength of him, so blissful to remember, to have again for ever now.

She murmured his name, felt her eyelids fluttering helplessly. She wanted only him, wanted everything he wanted, for all time.

And suddenly he was sweeping her up, leaping to his feet, whirling her around as if she were a feather, then striding off with her.

Breathless, she cried out, 'Nic! Where are you going?'

His eyes were alight with desire. With hunger for her. Urgent and possessing. 'To book us in to the lodge—right now!'

She gave another cry, half-laughing, half-rueful. 'Nic, it's closed for winter. It's day visitors only at this time of year.'

He lowered her abruptly, disbelievingly. She pressed herself against him, hugging him close. She was as light as the very air.

'We'll have to find somewhere outside the park,' she told him.

She stepped away, fishing her car keys from her purse. 'First person to reach a motel warms the bed!' she cried, and raced for the car park and her car.

He caught her before she'd even opened the door, sweeping her back to him.

'We'll take mine,' he said, brooking no argument. 'I'll send someone to collect yours. Because from now on…' his blue, blue eyes poured into hers, and what she saw in them melted her all the way down to her fast-beating heart '…wherever we go, my adored, Fran, we go *together*.'

He scooped her up, lowering her into his own hire car, then climbing in himself.

'Ready to start our next road trip?' he asked. His sapphire eyes were ablaze for her and her alone as he reached across to kiss her, to seal with her the union that they were making that would bind them one to each other, all their days. 'The one that will last a lifetime and beyond,' he said.

She gave a sigh of happiness and joy and a contentment that would never leave her. 'Let's go,' she said, 'wherever the road leads us.'

She smiled, with love in her eyes, her heart, her very being. Nic, *her* Nic, was hers for ever. The man she knew she loved and always would.

'Together...' she breathed. 'Always together.'

He gunned the engine, turning his flashing desert wolf smile at her, the one that turned her heart over and over.

'Sounds good to me,' he said, in the laconic, laid-back way she loved so much. He headed out towards the road. 'But we stop at the first motel we find, OK?'

His glinting glance at her, so rich with bone-melting promise, brooked no disagreement.

Fran laughed. As carefree as the wind.

'Definitely!' she agreed. 'The very first.'

EPILOGUE

THE VAST GREAT HALL at Beaucourt Castle, its bare stone walls bedecked with a fearsome array of medieval weaponry, was freezing— despite the half a tree trunk burning in the cavernous fireplace to one side.

Fran and Nic, newly arrived, walked up to the elderly man standing four-square by the hearth. As Fran kissed him on the cheek, then greeted her aunt, uncle and cousins, his gimlet eyes skewered the man standing beside her.

'So,' announced His Grace the Duke of Revinscourt, 'you think you're going to marry my granddaughter, do you?'

'Yes,' said Nic.

'Hmmph! Well, you've plenty of money, so I hear, but nothing of anything else!'

'No,' agreed Nic.

'Hotels, they tell me?' His Grace expanded.

'Yes,' said Nic again.

He was holding his ground. Fran had told

him to, but he'd have done it anyway. No way was he being put down. Not now. Not ever.

'And you intend to hold the wedding in one of them—is that it?'

'I didn't want to upstage Adrietta's wedding at home,' Fran put in. 'So Nic's given me the pick of all his properties.'

'She's opted for one that's on a private island in the Caribbean,' elaborated Nic.

'Caribbean? What's wrong with whatever you've got in town here? Mayfair, so I'm told—perfectly respectable!' the Duke expostulated irately.

'The Caribbean is warmer at this time of year,' Nic explained.

'Well, don't expect me to fly out there!' His Grace barked testily. 'Not at my time of life!'

'We understand that, Gramps,' Fran put in placatingly, not mentioning that that was exactly the reason her father had suggested it, knowing the occasion would be a lot more comfortable without the crotchety old Duke there. 'But we're holding an engagement party at the Falcone Mayfair, and of course we want you *there*.'

'Hmmph,' said His Grace—again. His eagle

eyes skewered his prospective grandson-in-law. 'Falcone, eh?'

His eyes lifted to the lofty armorial hatchment over the cavernous stone fireplace. Above the ducal coronet carved into the stone a fierce falcon hovered. Firelight glimmered on the same image on the Duke's signet ring. Then the grey eyes snapped back to Nic. Something in them had changed.

'Well, I don't hold with signs and portents, and I could do without you being another damned foreigner, like your father-in-law, but there it is. She'll do what she wants, this granddaughter of mine, just like her mother did. Marry who she wants and do what she wants. A doctor of astrophysics… What use is that, eh? Just like there's quite enough hotels in this world for my liking. But if the two of you want each other, that's enough. If you've come from nothing, then you've clearly got grit, and that counts for a lot.'

He shot a look towards his grandson, Harry, whose expression was a study as he tried to catch Fran's eyes and see her roll them along with his own at their grandfather's inquisition.

'And besides, this young idiot—who, one

day, God help us all, is going to be running this place— tells me he's going to rope you in for rugby.' The gimlet grey eyes turned approving and he nodded. 'Definitely a forward. Just what we need.'

Harry grinned, explaining, 'Castle versus village—the annual derby. Village always thrashes us. You, however, are going to be our secret weapon!'

'Happy to be of use,' replied Nic dryly.

His hand tightened on Fran's and she squeezed it back, throwing him a covert smile. He'd come through with flying colours, just as he had with her parents. Much to his astonished surprise.

Instead of the disdain and open disapproval he'd expected, the Marchese had shaken Nic vigorously by the hand, immediately asking his advice on how to transform an unused *palazzo* he happened to own into a luxury hotel.

As for Fran's young brother, Tonio—he'd declared it 'seriously cool' to have a brother-in-law with a police mugshot on file, and he couldn't wait to tell his cousin Harry. Fran's sister, Adrietta, had promptly informed him, with her prettiest smile, that she was determined to have her forthcoming honeymoon at the Falcone Seychelles, because she'd looked it up on the Internet and it was 'positively divine'.

As for her mother, Lady Emma, La Marchesa had simply exclaimed, 'Thank heavens Francesca's agreed to marry *someone* at last!' and warned Nic not to let her daughter jilt him, as was her habit with men she was engaged to.

'No, dearest Mama,' Fran had said sweetly, dropping a kiss on her mother's cheek. 'I won't be doing that. Because, you see, I love Nic and he loves me.'

Then, taking a breath, she'd explained the reason for her rush to the altar ahead of Adrietta.

Her surprise at her mother's reaction had equalled Nic's at her father's reaction to his becoming his son-in-law. A shriek of excitement had sounded from the Marchesa, accompanied by renewed vigorous pumping of Nic's hand by her father at the news that he and the Marchesa were to become grandparents.

With shock, Nic had realised that his presence in the di Ristori family was actually going to be *welcomed*.

It was a welcome that was being extended now by her maternal relatives too.

Fran's aunt, the Marchioness, had stepped forward. 'Come along, everyone! I am *not*,' she said decidedly, 'going to freeze here any longer if you are starting on about rugby! The drawing room is *much* warmer, and it's time to toast the happy couple!'

With quiet but practised management of her irascible father-in-law, she shepherded them through to where vintage champagne was awaiting them, installing the Duke in a vast winged chair by the fireside.

As Nic and Fran started to thaw they turned to each other.

'Told you Gramps would like you!' she whispered. 'Despite his manner, he likes people who aren't cowed by him. And I do so hope,' she said, 'that you will like them all too—all my family.'

He could see the emotion in her eyes and she made a little face.

'They really can't help being aristocrats, you know.' There was a mix of humour and wariness in her voice.

'I will do my best to ignore their unfortunate origins,' Nic promised her solemnly, for he would promise her the world now—and fetch it for her too.

For a moment Fran's expression wavered, then she landed a soft fist on his chest and laughed.

Emboldened, she added, 'Now all you have to do,' she gave a wry laugh '—apart from trying *not* to refer to Cesare as "the illustrious Conte" in that sardonic tone you always use about him—is make peace with Vito Viscari.'

This time his face darkened, his eyes hardening automatically.

But Fran held her ground. 'Nic, you can't go on feuding for ever. Vito isn't responsible for his having inherited the Viscari hotels, nor for his mother-in-law buying your half back, and nor was he responsible when his uncle handed him the management job you were after, way back when. Speaking of which...' she took a breath '... I've been putting my head together with Carla and Eloise—yes, I have, so don't make that face at me.'

Nic's expression was wary. 'And what have the three of you cooked up?' he enquired.

He had a feeling he was being outmanoeuvred, but for some strange reason—probably to do with the fact that he'd have laid down his life for the woman speaking to him, so much did he love her—he let her continue. Which she did.

'Well,' she said, encouraged, 'it's this…'

Her eyes gleamed with the same enthusiasm he was so familiar with when she talked about her beloved cosmology.

'We think the two of you—you and Vito—should start an international programme of apprenticeships for disadvantaged young people, just as *you* once were, Nic, and train them in all aspects of the hotel trade. Not just things like cheffing and housekeeping, but management and finance as well. Almost like a global university for the hospitality industry.'

Nic's eyes narrowed in consideration. 'The Falcone Foundation…' he mused. He liked the sound of it. Liked the concept.

'Well, I suppose it really ought to be the Viscari-Falcone Foundation,' Fran put in.

'You mean the Falcone-Viscari Foundation,' Nic corrected her.

Fran waved a hand. 'Whatever! You two can argue it out—or each have foundations of your own, if you insist. It doesn't matter. What matters is that you *co-operate*, Nic. You and Vito. For a common goal.' Her voice changed, softened. 'It's what brought you to what you are today—a man made good. Made very, *very* good.'

There was a little choke in her voice and Nic caught her hand, pressed his mouth against it, then against his heart. '*You've* made me good, *mio amore.*'

His eyes poured into hers and hers gazed up into his. She felt her heart flowering with the love she had for him. The rest of the world disappeared.

Then a voice beside them sounded. 'Save your canoodling for later, you two love birds, and have some champagne.'

Her aunt's voice was genial, and she was handing them two brimming flutes. Then, looking at her niece, she hesitated a moment.

'Should you?' she queried. 'I had a *very* excited phone call this morning from my sister-in-law. Telling me she's going to be a grandmother.'

'What's this?' Harry sauntered up, catching the last of the sentence. 'Fran—you're *never* preggers, are you? Wow, fast work, Falcone. Still, all the more champers for me!' he said cheerfully, helping himself to Fran's glass.

Then he looked across at Nic.

'Don't overdo it on the fizz tonight, old chap. There's a training session first thing tomorrow morning—we need to see what position is best for you. Put you through your paces. Dad and I are thinking forwards, definitely, but just where is the question. I'm thinking back row, so—'

Fran silenced him with a hand over his mouth. 'Shut up, Harry,' she said amiably.

'OK,' he said good-naturedly, removing her hand. 'So, tell me more about this private island for the wedding? Sounds cool. I can't wait to party there.'

Fran laughed. 'Well, you won't be partying with us, Harry. We'll be in the honeymoon *cabana* at the far end of the island! *Totally* private,' she warned with a smile.

Her uncle was approaching, bearing a glass of orange juice which Fran took gratefully. Then the Marquess called for silence. 'I believe my father has a few words to say,' he announced.

Immediately everyone dutifully turned towards the Duke, seated as if he were enthroned.

'Raise your glasses, if you please,' he instructed, in his must-be-obeyed fashion. Everyone duly did, apart from Fran and Nic. 'And now,' he continued, in his stentorian voice, belying his years and his frailty, 'I am formally welcoming the newest member to our family. He's shown the amazingly good sense to choose my granddaughter for his wife, and for that alone I approve of him.'

A ripple of laughter went around the room.

'As for my granddaughter—well...' His voice changed, and with a sense of shock Fran realised he was suppressing emotion. 'Any man who can start with nothing and end up with a great deal more than anyone in *this* family has must have something to him. And whatever that is my granddaughter has had the good sense to see it, want it, and wish to marry him for it.'

He took a breath, held all their eyes. Then gave his toast.

'To Francesca and her husband-to-be. And...' there was a discernible note of satisfaction in his voice now '…to my next descendant—my great-grandchild!'

There was a general echoing of his toast, with much joviality, especially on his grandson's part, and then Fran was turning towards Nic. Her eyes were lambent with the emotion that she would always feel for him. Joy. Pure, overwhelming, incandescent joy.

'To us, Nic. To you and me and our precious, precious baby. Together for *ever*.'

Nic's sapphire eyes were for her and her alone. 'To us both,' he breathed. 'To us *all*.'

And then his glass was tilting against hers, and hers to his, and their toast was simple.

'To love,' they said in unison.

As it always would be, now and for all eternity.

The sun was setting over the Caribbean. Nic and Fran stood hand in hand as the priest said to them the words that would unite them in holy matrimony.

In the little open-air chapel, just behind her, Fran could hear her mother sobbing quietly. She knew, too, that her father would not have a dry eye either. Apart from her elderly grandfather, the Duke, all her family were here, on her father's side and her mother's, and though she knew they were all here for them both, she had spoken quietly to Nic before the ceremony.

'I want this to be for your mother too, Nic—the mother who raised you to be the man you are now. Strong and courageous and determined. I want—' her voice had choked a little '—I want this to be, as well, for the father you never knew. We don't know, Nic, just what made him turn his back on you, and maybe there were reasons neither you nor your poor mother knew about, but one thing I do know…' her voice had been fervent '…is that *you* are going to be the father to *your* child—*our* child—that he should have been. *Your* child and its siblings yet to come will have a father to be so proud of. So beloved. We'll make that happen, Nic. You and I. Together. And whether our children grow up to be star-gazers like me, or hoteliers like you, or something completely different, we shall love them for all their lives. And we shall love each other too.'

Her words echoed now in his head as, with a smile, the priest said the words that every bride and groom longed to hear.

'You may kiss the bride.'

Which was just what Nic did—long and sweet and tender and passionate. And Fran, his bride, his beloved, beautiful bride, who took his breath away with every glance at her, kissed him right back as the golden glow of the setting sun bathed them both in its glorious light.

* * * * *

LET'S TALK
Romance

For exclusive extracts, competitions
and special offers, find us online:

- facebook.com/millsandboon
- @millsandboonuk
- @millsandboon

Or get in touch on 0844 844 1351*

For all the latest titles coming soon,
visit millsandboon.co.uk/nextmonth

Want even more
ROMANCE?

Join our bookclub today!

'Mills & Boon books, the perfect way to escape for an hour or so.'

Miss W. Dyer

'Excellent service, promptly delivered and very good subscription choices.'

Miss A. Pearson

'You get fantastic special offers and the chance to get books before they hit the shops'

Mrs V. Hall

Visit millsandbook.co.uk/Bookclub and save on brand new books.

MILLS & BOON